THE TEXAS TATTLER

All The News You Need To Know...And More!

Who could have imagined that confirmed Texas bachelor Lance Brody would return from a trip to Washington, D.C., engaged! And to a woman he'd never met before. The successful businessman claims it's a love match, but we certainly have our doubts. Miss Bea Cavanaugh is well-connected to all the people the Brody brothers need. We smell merger rather than marriage!

But we also don't see this "engagement" being a long one. Not that Lance is heading down the aisle soon. No, we've seen the looks he's been giving his personal assistant. Especially now that the formerly nondescript Miss Thornton has suddenly blossomed into a yellow rose of Texas. With the fiancée so far away, how soon before the groom-to-be starts to play?

Dear Reader,

Kate is a heroine who is very close to me. She's a bit of an ugly duckling in the beginning, someone who's very comfortable hiding who she is. She likes blending into the background and hoping that the man she loves will notice her. But when Lance Brody announces his engagement to another woman, Kate realizes it's time to take action. Kate is a woman in flux. I think most of us are. We are constantly changing and reinventing ourselves, trying to find an outer shell that matches the inner woman. For Kate this new sexier face and body she sees in the mirror is a stranger. And she has to find her confidence again.

This book is the start of six months of fun with the new millionaires of the TEXAS CATTLEMAN'S CLUB. They are a lot of fun. I hope you enjoy reading about them.

Happy reading!

Katherine

KATHERINE GARBERA

TAMING THE TEXAS TYCOON

Silhouette® Desire

Published by Silhouette Books

America's Publisher of Contemporary Romance

Special thanks and acknowledgment to Katherine Garbera
for her contribution to the Texas Cattleman's Club miniseries.

This book is dedicated to my mom and dad. I don't think I say thank you
enough or let you know just how lucky I am to have you as parents.
So...thank you, Mom and Dad. I love you very much.

Acknowledgments

I'd like to give a shout-out to the other authors
in the TEXAS CATTLEMAN'S CLUB series—Michelle, Brenda,
Charlene, Day and Jennifer. It was a lot of fun to write with you.

SILHOUETTE BOOKS

ISBN-13: 978-0-373-76952-0

TAMING THE TEXAS TYCOON

Recycling programs
for this product may
not exist in your area.

Books by Katherine Garbera

Silhouette Desire

The Bachelor Next Door #1104
Miranda's Outlaw #1169
Her Baby's Father #1289
Overnight Cinderella #1348
Baby at His Door #1367
Some Kind of Incredible #1395
The Tycoon's Temptation #1414
The Tycoon's Lady #1464
*Cinderella's Convenient
    Husband* #1466
Tycoon for Auction #1504
Cinderella's Millionaire #1520
††*In Bed with Beauty* #1535
††*Cinderella's Christmas
    Affair* #1546
††*Let It Ride* #1558
Sin City Wedding #1567
††*Mistress Minded* #1587
††*Rock Me All Night* #1672
†*His Wedding-Night Wager* #1708
†*Her High-Stakes Affair* #1714

†*Their Million-Dollar Night* #1720
The Once-A-Mistress Wife #1749
***Make-Believe Mistress* #1798
***Six-Month Mistress* #1802
***High-Society Mistress* #1808
**The Greek Tycoon's Secret
    Heir* #1845
**The Wealthy Frenchman's
    Proposition* #1851
**The Spanish Aristocrat's
    Woman* #1858
Baby Business #1888
§*The Moretti Heir* #1927
§*The Moretti Seduction* #1935
§*The Moretti Arrangement* #1943
Taming the Texas Tycoon #1952

††King of Hearts
†What Happens in Vegas…
**The Mistresses
*Sons of Privilege
§Moretti's Legacy

KATHERINE GARBERA

is a strong believer in happily-ever-after. She's written more than thirty-five books and has been nominated for career achievement awards in series fantasy and series adventure from *Romantic Times BOOKreviews*. Her books have appeared on the Waldenbooks/ Borders bestseller list for series romance and on the *USA TODAY* extended bestseller list. She loves to travel and lives in Dallas, Texas, with her two children and the man of her dreams. You can visit her on the Web at www.katherinegarbera.com.

The Texas Cattleman's Club

#1952 *Taming the Texas Tycoon*—
Katherine Garbera, July 2009

#1958 *One Night with the Wealthy Rancher*—
Brenda Jackson, August 2009

#1964 *Texan's Wedding-Night Wager*—
Charlene Sands, September 2009

#1970 *The Oilman's Baby Bargain*—
Michelle Celmer, October 2009

#1977 *The Maverick's Virgin Mistress*—
Jennifer Lewis, November 2009

#1983 *Lone Star Seduction*—
Day Leclaire, December 2009

One

"Brody Oil and Gas, Kate speaking," Kate Thornton said into the phone as she did about fifty times a day.

"Hey, Katie-girl, any fires I need to put out?" Lance Brody asked.

"Hi, Lance, how was DC?" she said while she sorted through the messages on her desk. Her boss was everything she'd ever wanted in a man and, embarrassingly for her, he never saw her as anything other than his ultra-efficient administrative assistant. Which was great—really it was. That's what she was paid for.

She'd joined Brody Oil and Gas shortly after Lance and his brother, Mitch, had inherited the failing refineries. And over the last five years, Lance and Mitch had turned their fortunes around and were now members of the famed Texas Cattleman's Club.

"DC was hot and the meetings were long. Messages?" Lance asked.

"You have two that aren't urgent but that you might want to handle before you get back to the office. One is from Sebastian Huntington regarding TCC business. Do you need his number?"

"Nah, I got it. What's the other one?"

"The other one is from Lexi Cavanaugh. I didn't recognize her name but she asked for you to call her as soon as you landed."

"She's my fiancée," Lance said.

Kate felt all the blood leave her body. She knew Lance was still talking because she could hear his voice beyond the buzzing in her ears. But all she could think was after years of secretly loving this man, he'd gone away and gotten engaged to someone she'd never even heard of.

"Katie-girl? You still there?"

"Yes," she said. "Of course I am. That's it on the messages. When do you think you'll be in the office?"

"En route now. The traffic on highway 45 is heavy, though. I need one more thing from you," he said.

Please don't ask me to plan your engagement party, she thought.

"Double-check with the caterers for Thursday's Fourth of July barbecue. I want to make sure this year's party blows the top off of last year's."

"No problem," she said, hearing her own voice break. She didn't know how she was going to be able to work with Lance every day now that he was clearly another woman's man.

"The other line is ringing," she said, though it wasn't. She just needed to get off the phone.

"I'll see you soon," he said, hanging up.

Kate hung up the phone and sat there staring at her computer screen. The wallpaper on her monitor was a photo of Lance, Mitch and her taken in February when Lance and Mitch had received word they were going to be accepted into the millionaire's club. She'd bought a bottle of champagne and the three of them had toasted the brothers' success.

Back then it had seemed fine that both Lance and Mitch thought of her as nothing more than an assistant. She had believed that one day Lance would see past her horn-rimmed glasses and cardigan sweaters to the woman beneath.

Clearly, that wasn't the case.

She leaned forward, looking at the photo and realizing that part of the problem lay with her. Her thick dark hair was pulled back in a sloppy braid and her glasses were a little big for her face. She'd lost weight last year—almost eighty pounds—and hadn't bothered to get new frames for her smaller face. In fact, all of her clothes were just the old ones. They were all faded and too big for her.

She looked like someone's maiden aunt, she thought.

Having grown up in the Houston, Texas, suburb of Somerset, she was aware that taking care with her appearance was an important thing if she was going to catch a man's attention. But being overweight had made everything she wore look, well, not very nice. So she'd stopped trying.

She reached out and brushed her finger over Lance's face, trying to convince herself that she would be fine as he planned his wedding. That she could stay here in this office, working for the man she loved while he lived his life.

But she knew she couldn't. The only way she was ever going to be happy with her life would be if she took control of it, the same way she'd taken control of her body by stopping her binge eating and focusing on making herself healthier.

There was really only one way for that to happen. She was going to have to quit her job at Brody Oil and Gas.

Lance wasn't in the best of moods considering he'd just gotten engaged, a day he knew that most men considered one of the happiest of their lives. But then he wasn't marrying for love; he was marrying to ensure the future of Brody Oil and Gas. He and Mitch had grown up in the fading dreams of their father, a man who'd let the Brody name get washed up and their wells dry out.

But with Mitch's financial genius and his skills—hell make that *luck* at finding mineral deposits and oil reserves—they'd turned around Brody Oil and Gas.

He was back in Houston now, which was a relief. He hated being away from home for any length of time. He liked his life the way it was. Liked the roughness of his roughneck oil workers, liked the comfy feeling his secretary Kate gave him and liked that he had a home at the oil refinery that he'd never found anywhere else.

Few people knew that their old man had drunk away his fortune. Mitch and he had borne the brunt of the old man's anger at the loss of that fortune.

He rubbed the back of his neck as he pulled his truck into the reserved parking spot at the offices of Brody Oil and Gas.

His cell phone rang as he was getting out of the truck. He checked the ID. "Hey, Mitch. What's up?"

"I'm going to have to stay in DC a bit longer to work out the rest of the deal we put in place with your engagement."

"No problem. Do you think you'll be back for the Fourth?"

"Of course."

"I invited Lexi to join me. I want her to start getting to know everyone here," Lance said.

"That sounds good."

"You know her better than I do," Lance added,

thinking of the woman he was going to marry. "I was thinking I should get her a little gift to say thanks for agreeing to marry me. Should I ask Kate, or do you think you could suggest something?"

There was silence on the line and Lance pulled the phone away from his ear to make sure he hadn't lost the connection. "If you have any thoughts, just shoot me an e-mail."

"I'll do that. When are you going to tell Kate that you're engaged?"

"Already did. Why?" Lance walked up toward the building.

"No reason," Mitch said.

"Do you think I should have waited until I announced it to the rest of the company?"

"No," Mitch said. "She's not like the rest of the staff."

"I know that. Do you think I should call Senator Cavanaugh to follow up on anything?"

"I'm handling that. Just keep doing what you usually do," Mitch said.

"And that is?" Lance asked.

"Heavy lifting," Mitch said.

Lance smiled. From the time they were very little, Mitch had relied on him to do the heavy physical stuff. It only made sense since he was the older brother, and Lance had learned early on that their parents weren't going to watch out for either of them.

"Will do. See you on Thursday?"

"Wouldn't miss it," Mitch said.

He disconnected the call and stood there for another moment in the hot, Houston sun. It might sound like he was daft to others but he liked the burn of the summer sun on his skin.

The air-conditioning chilled him as he walked through the building. There was always a moment when he almost paused as he entered the office, unable to believe how he and Mitch had brought the empty, run-down company back to this. The lobby was filled with guests waiting to go up to different meetings. There was a full staff of security guards who protected the company.

"Good afternoon, Mr. Brody."

"Good afternoon, Stan. How's things?"

"Good, sir. Good to have you back in Houston," Stan said.

Lance nodded at the man and walked toward the executive elevators. He got on and pushed the button for the executive floor. The ride was quick and he realized he was eager to be back to work. DC was like another world, a place he didn't fit in. Here at Brody Oil and Gas, he not only fit in, he was in his kingdom.

He walked into his office and Kate glanced up at him. Her normal smile of welcome wasn't as bright as it usually was.

"Welcome back, Lance. Steve from finance needs five minutes sometime today. I told him I had to check with you first."

"No problem. I'm free this afternoon."

"Good. I'll take care of it."

"Anything else I need to know about?"

She shook her head, a strand of her thick dark hair brushing her cheek. She looked up at him and her eyes seemed wider, those dark-chocolate orbs that he'd lost himself in a time or two. He shook his head. That was folly. Kate wasn't the type of woman who'd be interested in an affair.

And despite his engagement, affairs were all he'd ever been interested in. He wasn't the kind of man who could marry a woman he felt anything for. He'd learned from his father that Brody men didn't handle lust or love well. They required devotion and dedication from their lovers or else they turned to jealousy. He had experienced it himself during his ill-fated love affair with his high school sweetheart April, when he was eighteen.

"Lance?"

"Hmm?"

"Did you hear what I said?"

He shook his head. "No, I was thinking about the trip to DC."

Kate bit her lip and looked down.

"What is it, Katie-girl? Is something on your mind?"

Kate nodded. "I need a few minutes to talk to you in your office."

"Okay," he said. "Now?"

"Yes, I think the sooner we get to this the better."

"Come on in," he said.

She stood and picked something up from her printer before leading the way into his office. Lance watched her walking in front of him, seeing the sway of her hips and the way the fabric of her long skirt brushed her calves.

Why was he just now realizing that Kate was one fine-looking woman beneath those ugly clothes of hers?

* * *

Kate had been in Lance's office many times before and today she felt a pang at the paper she held in her hand. She had made up her mind that she was going to resign. There was nothing that could change that.

Well, that wasn't true. She vacillated between being firm that she had to leave, and wanting to stay so she could see Lance on a daily basis.

But then she had to remember that part of the reason she'd lost the weight was because she was tired of sitting on the sidelines of life, and watching other people live while she just went about doing her job and going home to her empty town house in Houston.

That emptiness had started getting to her and she'd contemplated buying a cat. But she'd stopped, horrified at becoming her great-aunt Jean, the spinster and butt of most jokes by the younger generation when Kate was growing up.

"What did you want to talk about?" Lance said. He leaned one hip on the front of his desk and stretched his long legs out.

She stared at him for a minute. How was she going to get over him?

"I have been thinking about my job lately.

And I...I've decided to pursue opportunities away from Brody Oil and Gas."

"What?" Lance asked, standing up. "Why now? We need you, Katie-girl."

Katie-girl. He called her that stupid nickname that made her feel like she was five years old. And like a sister to him. She realized that she'd let the relationship develop that way, happy to have at least some sort of affection from him.

"That's the problem for me, Lance, you don't really need me. You might have back in the beginning when you hired me, but now any efficient office manager will be able to handle this. I think we both know that."

"That's been true for the last two years. Why are you leaving now?"

She shrugged. She hadn't thought that Lance would care, to be honest. "It just seems like a good time to make a move. Everything is going well here, you're engaged and Mitch is spending more time in DC. A new person will be able to transition smoothly."

He rubbed the back of his neck. "Is anything the matter, Kate? Did I do something I shouldn't have?"

"Not at all. It's me, Lance. I keep staying here

year after year because it's comfortable, and I think we both know that isn't the way to really have a successful career."

"Is that what this is about? We can promote you into a different role," he said.

She shook her head. "No. Thank you for the offer but I'm ready to try something new."

Kate was tempted to say yes to anything that Lance suggested, but she refused to let go of the fact that he was getting married, and to stay here…well, it would be the dumbest thing she could ever do.

"Will you stay until I can hire a replacement?"

She nodded. That sounded fair to her. "Of course I will."

"Thanks for that."

"I guess…here is my resignation. I'll be at my desk if you need anything else from me."

She turned to leave and felt as if she was running away. A part of her wondered if she shouldn't try to stay here and make things different between her and Lance. But how?

She'd Googled Lexi Cavanaugh as soon as Lance had told her about the engagement, and there was no way that she could compete with a woman like that.

"Kate?"

"Yes, Lance."

"I would like to have a cake at the barbecue to celebrate my engagement to Lexi. Can you order one from the bakery for me?"

"Of course," she said.

It was definitely time for her to leave Brody Oil and Gas.

She realized that she and Lance hadn't hammered out the details of her leaving the company. "I'll stay for two weeks."

"It might take longer than that to hire your replacement."

"I'd like to try to fit it into that time schedule," she said.

"Have I done something to upset you, Kate? You know I'm more of a roughneck than an executive," he said.

She steeled herself against responding to that rough aw-shucks-ma'am charm that he was able to pull off so easily. She liked that he wasn't as sophisticated and polished as Mitch was. That was why she'd fallen for him. At heart, Lance was a good old boy, a Texas man like her daddy and her brothers. The kind of guy that knew how to charm the pants off any lady.

And he hadn't had to work hard to win her affections. But she realized now that the charm was just part of his practiced act. It was as much a part of the savvy millionaire as his thousand-dollar cowboy boots and million-dollar mansion. He pulled out the charm when he needed it.

"No, Lance. You didn't do anything other than treat me like your secretary."

"Is that a problem?" he asked, his shrewd gaze on her.

"Not at all. But that's all I am to you and I decided I want more."

She walked out of his office and closed the door behind her. She knew she should stay and work the rest of the day but she needed to get away. And she didn't care if it made her seem cowardly. She went downstairs and put the top down on her Miata convertible and drove out of Houston, leaving Brody Oil and Gas behind. She only wished it were as easy to convince her heart to leave Lance Brody in the dust.

Two

Lance was speechless as Kate not only walked out of his office, but left early. He knew he'd missed something important as far as she was concerned. She said she wanted to be more than his secretary—did she mean professionally, or personally?

He started to go after her but realized he had no idea where she went when she left the offices. To be honest, she was always here when he arrived and she stayed until after he left. How was he going to operate without her? Kate *was* more than just his secretary. She was the most important piece of the office, the person who kept everything running smoothly and kept him in line.

"Damn it," he said to no one in particular. He hadn't gotten to where he was by letting things like this go. He speed-dialed her cell phone.

"I can't talk now, Lance," she said.

"Then pull over or use the headset I gave you, because you can't just walk away like that and expect me to let this go."

"Hold on," she said. He heard her fumbling around and then cursing, and a minute later she was back. "What do you want to talk about?"

"The fact that you left like you did."

"I'm sorry," she said. "That was so unprofessional, but I just didn't think I could be productive anymore today."

"I can understand that. Want to tell me why?"

"No. It'll just make you uncomfortable and make me feel like a big dummy."

Lance didn't like the sound of that. "Kate, if I've done something, just flat out tell me. I'll apologize and we can move on."

"I don't think we can," she said. Her words were sad and he wished she were still in the office so he could see her expressions. Kate had the most expressive eyes of any woman he'd ever met.

"You won't know until we talk," Lance said. He would fix this problem with Kate—he couldn't afford to lose her. "Where are you?"

"On the interstate headed toward Somerset."

"Going to your parents house?" he asked, knowing that Kate had grown up in Somerset, a wealthy suburb of Houston. He had a house there now.

"I guess so. I just got in the car and kind of drove on autopilot. I didn't realize where I was headed."

"Katie-girl—"

"Don't call me that, Lance. It makes me feel like we have a relationship beyond boss-secretary and I know that's not true."

He cursed under his breath. "We do have one. We're friends, Kate. And we have been all these long years."

"Are we really friends?"

"Of course we are. We are more than friends…you're like part of the family to Mitch and me, and to be honest, Kate, I don't think either of us will know what to do without you."

She was quiet for a few seconds.

"Kate?"

"I just can't talk about this anymore, Lance. I know to you it probably seems…how does it seem?"

"Like I've done something to upset you. Listen, whatever it is, I can fix it. You know that, right?"

"You can't."

"Kate, when have we ever encountered a problem or obstacle that I couldn't figure a way out of?"

"Lance…"

She was weakening as he'd known she would. His other line was ringing and he ignored it.

"Tell me, Kate."

"I'm not sure I can. I feel silly that you are making such a big deal out of it now," she said.

One of the first things he'd liked about Kate was her voice. It was soft and sweet and even when she got mad, which wasn't often, she kept it pleasant.

"Why don't you come back to the office and we can talk," Lance said.

"We can talk tomorrow when I come in. I think I need the night to get my mind together."

Lance knew it was important to get Kate back

and convince her to stay on before too much time had passed. He knew that she could find other jobs that would pay her as much as he did. But he needed her.

The other line started ringing again and his cell phone beeped with a text message from Frank Japlin, the head of operations at their main refinery.

"Kate, can you hold on a minute?"

"What?"

"I've got to take a call from the refinery," he said.

"Sure," she said.

He put her on hold and answered the call. "It's Brody."

"Frank here. We have a fire at the refinery. I think you need to get down here right away."

"Have you called the fire department?"

"First thing. But this blaze is burning to beat the band."

"I'm in the middle of another emergency."

"There is a lot of damage. And I heard one of the investigators say they thought the cause of the fire wasn't accidental."

Great. Just what he needed today. "See what else you can find out. I'll give you a call in fifteen minutes or so."

"Okay, boss," Frank said, hanging up.

Lance rubbed the back of his neck, thinking that damage was the last thing they needed at the refineries. The hurricane they'd had last fall had already done enough damage to them.

He needed Kate back in her chair, taking care of this mess. He'd have to call the press, the families and the insurance company. He glanced down at his phone and noticed that the line where she'd been holding was now off. She'd hung up.

Just what he needed, he thought.

Kate realized, as she was hanging on the phone waiting for Lance, that she'd spent too much of her time in that static role. Lance had gotten engaged. There was nothing he could say or do that was going to make staying on at Brody Oil and Gas okay.

She hung up the call and kept on driving. Going home to her folks' place wasn't the smartest idea. Her mom would just tell her that if she wore makeup and dressed nicer, she wouldn't still be single. And honestly, who could deal with that?

But she didn't want to go to her town house and spend the night alone. She needed some good advice. She needed to be with her best friend, Becca Huntington. Becca would commiserate with her and tell her not to go back, not to listen to Lance…wouldn't she?

She called Becca at Sweet Nothings, the lingerie shop she owned in Somerset.

"Sweet Nothings."

"Becca, it's Kate."

"Hey, there. How's things in the big city?" Becca asked.

"Horrible."

"What? Why?"

"Lance is engaged."

Becca didn't say anything for a moment and Kate realized she probably seemed like a loser to her friend. "Oh, honey, I'm sorry. I didn't realize he was dating anyone."

"He wasn't."

"Are you sure he's engaged? Lance doesn't strike me as the kind of guy who'd do something that spontaneous."

He wasn't spontaneous and he was careful not to be tied down by any of the women he got involved with. "Yes, he told me the news himself."

"Who is she?"

"Lexi Cavanaugh."

"Senator Cavanaugh's daughter?"

"Yes."

"Is it politically motivated?" Becca asked.

"I don't know. And I don't care. I quit my job."

"You did what?"

"Was that crazy? I'm so confused, I don't know what to do," Kate admitted. She'd hoped that Lance would realize she was waiting there and fall for her.

"It may have been a little crazy. I know you've had a bit of a crush on him," Becca said.

Kate took a deep breath. "It's more than a crush. I'm in love with him."

It was the first time she'd said the words out loud, and she had to admit they felt good. Or they would have if Lance wasn't engaged to another woman."

"Oh, Kate."

"He doesn't even know I'm a woman.

"Let's fix that," Becca said.

"How?"

"Come to the shop and we'll give you a makeover."

"A makeover? I don't think so. Remember the last time we tried."

Kate had felt so uncomfortable in the makeup and clothing that Becca had suggested, she'd ended up going straight home and taking it all off. She needed the comfort of her old clothing…or did she?

"I just don't know what to do," she repeated.

"Only you can figure that out. But if it were me, I'd change my hair and my clothes. Just start over and find a new love."

"I have to work for Lance for two more weeks."

"Why?"

"I couldn't just quit and walk out on him."

"All the better," Becca said. "You can go back to work looking like a million bucks and then leave. It will be a chance to get back a little of your pride."

Would her pride feel any better if she came back to Brody Oil and Gas and Lance looked at her like a woman instead of his assistant?

"I'm coming to your shop," Kate said.

"Good, we can talk once you get here. I'll have the white wine chilled."

"Thanks, Becca."

"For what?"

"Being here. Listening to me and not thinking I'm being silly."

"Why would I think you're silly? I've been in love before and I know what it can do to you."

Kate swallowed, glad she had a friend like Becca to turn to. "I've never loved anyone before Lance."

"Not even in high school?"

"I had a crush or two," Kate admitted.

They'd been friends for what seemed like forever and Becca had always been the sister she'd never had—the one person who accepted her the way she was. At home, her brothers teased her if she did anything girly and her mother was never satisfied with any of the choices that Kate made.

"That was different. And don't ask me why. I can't explain it, but Lance Brody has always been different."

"I know he has. I've never heard you talk about one person as much as you do him."

"Am I annoying?"

Becca laughed, and the familiar sound of it made Kate smile.

"No, you aren't annoying. Just in love. I'm sorry that he didn't turn out to be the guy you hoped he would be."

Kate was, too. "Maybe he is that guy, but just not the one for me."

"Probably," Becca said. "When will you be here?"

"In about twenty minutes. I just left work without asking or anything."

"I think you're ready for a change," Becca said.

"Why?"

"Because you're already acting like a rebel."

Kate thought about that. "I guess I am. Maybe Lance's engagement will turn out to be good for me."

"I bet it will. If not you'll be stronger for having loved and lost him."

Kate hung up the phone and continued driving toward Somerset. She didn't think about Lance or Brody Oil and Gas. She just concentrated on herself and the new woman she was becoming. It was way past time for her to change.

It was hot and smoky at the refinery. The fire burned for almost three hours before the firefighters got it under control. Frank was busy talking to local media and Lance was calling his brother. Mitch was in a meeting and Lance had to leave a voice mail.

"Catch me up on what's going on," Lance said to Frank.

"We have four injured."

"Have you talked to their families?"

"As soon as we identified the men who'd been injured. They're in the emergency room now. I sent JP down there to talk to the families and make certain that there were no questions as to insurance coverage, et cetera. And I asked him to keep me posted on any pressing health issues," Frank said.

"Good. Do you think we're going to have to shut down?"

Frank rubbed the top of his balding head. "I won't know more until we have a chance to talk to the fire chief."

"When will that be?"

"Soon, I hope."

"Have you stopped the flow of oil into the refinery?"

"First thing we did. We enacted our emergency protocols. And everything went exactly as it should have. I'm going to send you some suggestions for commendation for some of our guys who went beyond the call of duty."

"I'll look for that," Lance said. His cell phone rang and he glanced at it. "It's Mitch."

"I'll go see if I can talk to the fire chief," Frank said.

"We've had a fire at the main refinery," Lance told Mitch.

"Is everyone okay? How bad is the damage?" Mitch asked.

Lance caught him up. "Do you think this will impact the senator's plan to allow us more drilling?"

"Not if I have anything to say about it. I'm going to go to his office right now."

"I'll get this under control. I'm going to have a press conference later on to let everyone know we're okay and still in business."

"Sounds good. I'll get back with you after I've spoken to the senator."

Lance hung up with his brother and surveyed the mess at the refinery. Employees were clustered to one side, all of them waiting to see what the verdict would be. They were a 67,000-barrel-a-day refinery, and if they had to shut down, all of those people would be without work. And they wouldn't make their quarterly revenues.

He dialed Kate's number. She usually served as a hub during these kinds of emergencies, when he couldn't be in the office.

Her phone went to voice mail and he realized that she was serious about leaving the company. "It's Lance. I need your help. We've had a fire at our main refinery. Call me when you get this message."

The receptionist at the Brody Oil and Gas office wasn't experienced enough to handle all the calls that were coming in. But the secretaries who worked for his duty managers could. Lance usually relied on Kate to take care of liaising with them. Guess it was time to figure out how to work without Kate. He called the finance manager and asked him to send every secretary they had down to help out. He then composed a short memo on his BlackBerry and sent it to the entire company apprising them of the situation and telling them that no one was authorized to speak to the media.

Frank waved Lance over to where he was with the fire chief.

"Lance Brody, this is Chief Ingle," Frank said.

"Thanks for getting the fire under control so quickly," Lance said, shaking the fire chief's hand.

"You're welcome. It is our job."

"I know that. But I'm grateful all the same. What are we looking at here?" Lance asked him.

"We thought it was started by an explosion, but we've been talking to the men closest to the location where the fire started and none of them reported hearing one," Chief Ingle said.

"That's odd. How do you think the fire started?" Lance asked.

"I've called for our fire-scene investigators to do a thorough examination of the area. But one of my men thought he saw cans of fire accelerant."

"What kind?"

"We don't have any details but I wanted you to know what we suspected. I've called the arson investigator and he's sending his team out, as well."

"Crap. I have to notify our insurance company. They will want to work with your arson team."

Chief Ingle nodded. "They always do."

Insurance companies were very well versed in arson investigations—they didn't mess around with fires. Lance wanted someone who had Brody Oil and Gas's interests in mind. "Is it okay if I hire my own security team to be part of the investigation?"

"We'd rather not have extra people on the site," Chief Ingle said.

"Darius won't get in the way. He's the best at what he does."

"Darius who?"

"Darius Franklin. He owns his own security firm."

"Okay, but only him."

Lance understood that. The chief didn't want a bunch of men trampling over the fire scene.

"When can we go back into production?" Lance asked.

"I think we'll need at least 24 hours before I'd feel comfortable saying you can go back on line. More, if the investigation proves to be complicated."

Lance made a note of that. And when the chief moved on, he turned to Frank. "Tell all of our employees to gather in the parking lot in fifteen minutes. Then set up a number so they can call in and get a message about when to report back to work and give them that number."

"I'm on it," Frank said, walking away.

Lance dialed his best friend, Darius, and got his voice mail. Being as succinct as possible, he told Darius what had happened, that the fire chief suspected arson, and he asked Darius to come and help with the investigation. Now if he could just get Kate back, he'd have the best team any man could ask for in this situation. He reached for his phone.

Three

Kate put her phone on silence after the second call from Lance. She was tired of hurting and questioning herself and everything she'd done. She arrived at Sweet Nothings to find that Becca had made her an appointment with her hairstylist.

"I don't know that a haircut is going to change anything," Kate said.

"Don't think of it as just a haircut. You need to change," Becca said. "I've been thinking about this since you called and the only way you are going to be able to make these next few weeks bearable is to make Lance Brody realize what he's missing."

Kate took one look at herself in the mirror behind the counter and shrugged. "Not much."

"Soon, he'll see a whole new woman."

"But I'll still be me," Kate said.

"Of course you will, silly. And Lance already likes you. This will just make him lust after you."

"He's engaged to be married, Becca."

"So what? You're not going to make him do anything. Just tease him a bit and maybe get your heart back."

Kate liked the sound of that. She'd given Lance five years. And wasn't it past time to get over him?

"Okay. I'll do it."

"Good."

Becca gave her directions to the salon. As Kate drove over there, her cell phone rang again. It was Lance. She answered the call as she parked her car. "It's Kate."

"Where have you been?"

"Driving," she said.

"There's been a fire at our main refinery. I need you in the office to be my information hub."

Kate was shocked. Brody Oil and Gas was one of the safest refineries in the business. "Was there an explosion?"

"They aren't sure. I'm done looking over the fire scene at the refinery. When can you get to the office?"

She almost said tonight, but what was the point of that? This was an emergency situation but they didn't really need her. Paula and Joan, two of the other secretaries at Brody Oil and Gas, could handle the phones in this situation.

"Tomorrow morning," she said.

"Kate, I need you."

Her heart almost skipped a beat.

"The company needs you. This is one of those times when we really want to have our best players on the field."

Lance had played football and she had noticed early on that he fell back on sports analogies when he was stressed.

"You've got your best players," she said. "I'm being traded, remember?"

"Damn it. We haven't decided that yet."

"Yes, we have. Or maybe I should say I have. I will call Paula and make sure she's prepared to collect information and disseminate it. I made a procedure file for this type of emergency after the hurricane last year."

Lance didn't say anything. "I guess that'll have to do. Leave your phone on so I can get in touch with you."

"Why? I'm not—"

"Stop arguing with me, Kate. I don't like it. What's gotten into you?"

She looked at herself in the rearview mirror and realized this was the first time she'd ever said no to Lance. And he didn't like it. Maybe the way to get his attention was actually easier than changing her hair and clothes. She realized that she'd been too accommodating, and that was part of the reason he'd taken her for granted.

"I don't know, Lance. I just decided it was time for a change. Don't make this into anything other than that."

"It feels like…"

"What?"

"Nothing," he said. "Will you be in the office tomorrow?"

"Yes, I'll be there."

"Good," Lance said.

"I'm sorry about the refinery," she said, feeling bad because of the way he sounded. "Were there injuries?"

"Four men are at the hospital now."

"I'll have Paula send flowers to them and food baskets to their families."

"Thanks," he said.

"You're welcome." She felt a little guilty about not going in and taking care of the details herself, but Lance and she both needed to get used to other people working for him because Kate couldn't continue to be his Girl Friday *and* be in love with him. That was the path to pain and destruction for her. And she was tired of living for the few brief moments when she and Lance were in the office together.

"Goodbye, Lance," she said, hanging up the phone. She sat in the car for another minute but the heat was getting to her. Or at least that was what she told herself. She didn't want to think that the idea of being without Lance was causing her to feel light-headed.

Lance spent the rest of the afternoon and most of the evening at the main refinery. Darius had arrived late and had agreed to stay and work with the fire investigators. Since he wasn't an arson investigator per se, all Darius could really do was narrow down the list of suspects and conduct investigations into the backgrounds of those who might have had probable cause to start the fire.

Lance left the refinery and drove back toward Houston deciding that he was ready for a new day. This one had been too…crazy, he thought.

When he'd been a boy, he'd longed for a busy day so he wouldn't have time to go home or to think about the home he had waiting for him. But that was long ago, he thought. Now he lived alone and liked it that way.

Well, he lived alone for now. Soon he'd be bringing a bride to his mansion in Somerset and he wasn't sure he was ready to try suburban living with a wife yet. But he and Mitch had agreed he was the one who should marry Lexi.

Damn, he thought, rubbing the back of his neck. Tension seemed to take up residence there when things weren't going well.

His cell phone rang and he checked the caller ID before answering it.

"Hello, Mitch."

"Hey, big bro. How are things at the refinery?"

"A mess, but I have Darius working with the fire investigators to try to make sense of it. How's DC?"

Mitch let out a long breath. "It could be worse. I handled most of it with Senator Cavanaugh's office. Let them know the proactive things that Brody Oil and Gas are doing to minimize damage to the community and the environment. I think that helped to soothe his fears over backing expanding oil production."

"Did you tell him that with additional refineries we could rotate operations so the loss of this one for a day wouldn't impact oil prices?" Lance asked.

"Yes, I did. I'm watching the markets as they open in Japan. I think we will see US crude prices jump."

"I know we will. With the economy being what it is, that's the last thing we need right now."

"We can't control the actions of investors," Mitch said.

"I am stopping by the hospital on my way home. I think it'd be a good idea for you to call the injured workers—I'll send you a text with their names when I'm done."

"All right, that sounds good. Lexi and I are going to fly back to Houston together tomorrow."

"I haven't had a chance to talk to her. She called me earlier. Will you let her know that until the mess at the refinery settles down, I can't talk?"

"Sure thing," Mitch said.

"Did you come up with any ideas for a gift yet?" Lance asked.

"Not yet. I haven't been thinking about your love life."

Lance hadn't been, either. "This is business, Mitch. Remember, you told me that. We need the Cavanaugh connection. Today proves that."

Mitch didn't add anything to that. And Lance had to guess that being a brilliant strategist meant his brother wasn't surprised that his planning had worked to their advantage.

"I forgot to mention that Kate gave her notice today."

"She did? Why?"

"She thinks this will be a good time for her transition out of her job with us. She's not being challenged enough or something like that."

"Maybe it is time she moved on."

"I'm trying to convince her to stay," Lance said.

"Why?"

Lance didn't know, but there was no way in hell he'd admit it. "She's part of the Brody Oil and Gas family and we need her."

"Maybe she wants to be more."

"Like how?" Lance asked remembering Kate's comment earlier.

"Think about it," Mitch said. "I've got to run. Don't forget to send me the names of the injured men."

"I won't. Ally got them interviews on the morning shows for tomorrow. She's going to talk to the families and prep them on what to say."

"Good. I'll advise the senator of this so maybe he can get a sound bite in, as well."

"This could have been a lot worse," Lance said.

"Why wasn't it?" Mitch asked.

"I think because of all the preparedness we worked on after the hurricane last fall. The guys really knew what to do and how to handle things."

Lance pulled into the hospital parking lot and chatted a few more minutes with his brother before hanging up. He didn't like hospitals. Never had, to be honest. Maybe because he'd visited more than his share of emergency rooms as a child.

His father had always been blunt in the parking lot. Telling him what to say when the doctors

asked about how he'd broken his arm or his leg—
bicycle accident; how he'd hurt his ribs or broken
his fingers—skateboard accident. Never did he
tell anyone the truth. And after a while, Lance realized even he kind of believed his dad's stories.

He rubbed his hand over the scars on the back
of his left knuckles. Some days he felt damned
old, older than his years. He knew he had to be
careful with Lexi. Had to remember to keep the
engagement and their eventual marriage man-
ageable.

Lance was always conscious that he'd inherited his father's legendary temper. And as he sat
in his truck looking at the modern hospital, he
couldn't help but remember the promise he'd
made to himself when he was thirteen. The
promise that he'd never bring a child of his to the
emergency room, because he'd never have children.

He wondered if that was going to be an issue
for Lexi Cavanaugh. A part of him hoped it
would be so he could end the engagement and
get his life back to the way it had been.

Kate was nervous as she got of out of her car
the next morning. Last night the new clothes

she'd purchased with Becca in Houston had seemed fun and daring but this morning when she'd put on the slim-fitting sundress and styled her new hair, she'd felt like an imposter.

It had taken her three tries to get her contacts in but at last she had her look as close as possible to the way the stylist had done it last night.

But she was nervous…and babbling, she thought. She always talked to herself but this morning her internal talk bordered on inane.

It all boiled down to one thing. What if everyone saw her and laughed?

Wasn't that silly? She was a grown woman and shouldn't care what anyone else thought but she was trying a new look—one that she was not certain of, despite Becca's reassurances that she looked *hot*. Kate still felt like fat, frumpy Kate, trying to be someone she wasn't.

She walked into the lobby, and Stan the security guard looked up. "Good morning…."

"Morning, Stan," she said, feeling awkward as the older gentleman just kept staring at her.

"You look nice today, Miss Thornton," Stan said. "Real pretty."

"Thank you, Stan," she said, the warmth of a blush on her cheeks.

She scanned her ID card and went to the executive elevator. While she waited, she stared at her reflection in the polished, mirrored wall that surrounded the elevator bank.

The hardest part about this makeover was that she simply didn't recognize herself.

"Excuse me, miss, but this elevator is for executive personnel only," Lance said, coming up behind her.

She turned around.

"Kate?"

She waited to see if he'd say anything else, but he didn't. That hurt a little bit but it was okay. Last night she'd decided to stop trying to please Lance, something that she'd done without much thought for a long time.

"I saw the workers on the *Today* show this morning. I thought they sounded good."

"Ally did a good job of prepping them. I'm glad they will all make a full recovery," Lance said.

The elevator car arrived and he waited for her to enter. She felt his eyes on her back as she moved in front of him. Was the skirt too short for the office?

But when she turned and saw him staring at

her legs, she realized that the dress was having its desired effect on him. He was finally seeing her as a woman. Kate felt…weird, actually.

Lance's attention was the one thing she'd craved and now she had it. But she wasn't sure what to do with it.

"How was your night?" she asked.

"I spent most of it on the phone…something that would have been easier if my assistant had been here."

She pursed her lips. "Maybe your assistant decided it was time to get herself a life."

"Did you, Kate? Is that what this is all about?"

She shook her head. "I've been ignoring myself for too long. I know my timing stunk last night but I had no idea there would be a fire at the main refinery."

"Who could have known? I don't mind if you take an afternoon off. In fact, if it would convince you to stay then I think we could work out more time off in your schedule," Lance said.

The elevator arrived at their floor and once again he gestured for her to go in front of him. As she walked past him, she heard him inhale sharply.

"Are you wearing perfume?" he asked.

She raised both eyebrows at him. "I am."

He shook his head. "Sorry. It's a very nice scent."

"Thank you," she said. Her new look seemed to be bothering Lance. Or maybe he just wasn't himself this morning. "I can handle the office this morning if you want to go back to the refinery."

"Thanks, Kate, but I think I am needed here. Especially if you are determined to quit."

She nodded and entered her office. The voice - mail light on her phone was flashing and she imagined she had a lot of messages waiting for her.

Lance closed the door and brushed past her to go into his office, knocking her off balance in the one-inch heels she was wearing. Lance steadied her with a hand on her waist. She turned her head and her hair brushed his shoulder.

Lance smelled good this morning but then she had always liked the scent of his aftershave. He put his other hand on her shoulder and looked down at her.

"I never realized how pretty your brown eyes are," he said.

She flushed. "I guess you couldn't really see them behind my glasses."

"Or maybe I never looked," Lance said.

"I think that there wasn't anything to look at before," Kate said. Becca had made a good point last night when she'd said that Kate hid behind her clothes and glasses.

"You are always worth a second look, Kate."

"Really?"

"Yes. I'm sorry I didn't notice before now."

"Why sorry?"

"Because you are so damned pretty."

"It's not me, it's the haircut and makeup," she said, uncomfortable with the compliment. She started pointing out all the things her mom had always told her were wrong with her. "My mouth is too big for my face."

He shook his head, rubbing his thumb over her bottom lip. "Your mouth is perfect for your face. Very lush and tempting…."

"Tempting? It's me, Lance. Kate Thornton. You've never thought I was tempting before."

"I must have been blind, Kate, because you are tempting me now," he said, lowering his mouth to hers. He kissed her.

She rose on her tiptoes and kissed him back. The moment was everything she'd imagined it would be and also completely unexpected. There was no way she could have imagined the way he tasted as his tongue slid over hers. Or the feel of his big hands in her hair. Or the way that one kiss could change her life completely.

Four

Kate tasted like heaven. She was pure temptation in his arms and he knew he'd never get enough of her. He didn't want to.

He slid his hands down the sides of her body. How had he missed this curvy body and those big, pretty eyes? Glasses and baggy clothes be damned, he'd have to have been blind to not see what a hottie his secretary was.

He turned to lean on the edge of her desk and pulled her more fully against him. Her breasts were full and felt good against his chest. He angled his head for deeper access to her mouth. He wanted more. He couldn't get enough of the taste of her. How had he missed this Kate all these years?

He lifted his head, rubbed his lips over hers and realized her eyes were closed. She looked so innocent in his arms. He remembered that he was a man who'd never learned how to handle the softer things in life. Having a lover was one thing, but this could never go beyond the physical.

As he traced the line of her face with her hair hanging free, he realized how delicate she was. "Should I apologize for that kiss?"

She opened her eyes and looked dazed for a moment but then she recovered. "Do you want to?"

"Not at all. I want to do it again but I don't think the office is the place for it."

"I agree."

His line rang, and Kate smiled at him as she reached over to answer it. "Brody Oil and Gas, Kate speaking."

Her smile faded. "Please hold."

"Who is it?"

"Your fiancée. You probably want to take that in your office."

Lance nodded. He didn't like that Lexi had interrupted his moment with Kate but he couldn't ignore her again.

"We're not done talking," Lance said.

"Of course not. We have the next two weeks to get through," Kate said, pulling out her chair and sitting down.

"When I'm done I want to see you in my office," he said. He wasn't going to pretend there wasn't a fierce attraction between them, but he didn't know how to deal with this new Kate who argued with him and didn't just do everything the way he wanted her to.

"Sure thing. You better go, you don't want to keep your fiancée waiting."

He pivoted on his heel and walked away from her. He went to his desk, sprawling in his leather chair. He reached for the phone and picked up the line where Lexi was holding.

"Hi, there, Lexi."

"Hi, Lance. I know you must be busy this morning but I wanted to thank you for the invitation to come to your Fourth of July party. I wanted to know what you need from me as your hostess."

Lance hadn't thought about Lexi acting as

hostess. "My secretary has taken care of all the details."

"I'll give her a call and see if I can help with anything. I think if we are going to make our marriage work, I should be involved with Brody Oil and Gas."

"Why?" Lance asked.

"Because that's where you spend all of your time," she said. "I know what it takes to be a good wife. You need a partner who can understand where you are coming from."

Lance knew that was the truth. But he didn't want Lexi here. He realized with a shock that when he thought of a partner—a female partner—at Brody Oil and Gas, he thought of Kate.

Why hadn't he realized that he wanted her before this? It was too late to change the past but he wanted to make things different between them going forward. But Kate didn't want any part of the company anymore and he was engaged to Lexi. He needed to sort this mess out. Was he going to try to make the match with Lexi work? And where did that leave Kate?

Mitch and Lance had determined that the connection to Cavanaugh was needed. And Lance had always put Brody Oil and Gas before everything else. He knew exactly what he needed to do, and how he needed to act. This was his chance to prove he wasn't the bastard his father had been.

He needed to be a better man. A man who wouldn't kiss Kate unless he could make a commitment to her. A man who would honor his commitment to Lexi. A man who was proud of who he was.

"You don't need to do anything for the picnic, but we can talk when you get here. Kate—my secretary—has given her two-weeks notice. If you are serious about wanting to be more involved, the picnic would be a great time for you to talk to her about the details of our events."

"I am serious, Lance. I want to make our marriage work."

There was a sincerity in Lexi's words that shamed him. He'd asked her to marry him and it was time to step up and honor that.

"I'll see you tomorrow," Lance said.

"I'm looking forward to it. Mitch has raved about the Brody Oil and Gas Fourth of July party."

"It's the one time of year when we pull out all

the stops for our workers. When we were re-building the business we decided that if we were going to be successful, we had to make everyone who worked for us feel like they were a part of the Brody Oil and Gas family."

"If your success is any indication, I'd say you've achieved that."

But at what cost? Mitch was determined and a workaholic just like Lance was. And this mar-riage wasn't real—it was purely business. Lexi was just another step in their plan to be success-ful. Was that any way to go through life, espe-cially when he had a woman like Kate on his hands? What was he doing?

Kate couldn't believe she'd lost her head and let Lance kiss her. It was wonderful…incredible, really, but so stupid. She was here to get over him. She was supposed to be using these two weeks to put him in her past.

She wanted to go out looking her best and she supposed she could count herself successful on that item. Lance hadn't even recognized her.

The sad part about that was she hadn't done anything except wear clothes that fit her. What a difference new clothes made. She would never have believed it. Mainly because her mother had been the one to say clothes made the man, and that woman had been wrong about so many things.

She glanced down at the phone and saw that Lance was still on the line with Lexi Cavanaugh. She knew next to nothing about the woman. But at the end of the day, Kate felt she'd owe Lexi a word of thanks.

If it hadn't been for that woman's engagement to Lance, Kate might have stayed stuck in her frumpy rut until she died an old lady spinster.

A wolf-whistle brought her head up as Marcus Wall walked into the office. He was one of the petroleum geologists who worked for them, one of the men who helped decide where Brody Oil and Gas drilled and he was an expert at picking the right location for their wells. "Dang, Kate, you look good today."

She smiled at him. "Thanks."

"I never noticed how big your eyes were before," he said, coming into her office and leaning on her desk. He must have come into the office at least a hundred times before and he'd never sat close or really even talked to her.

She wanted to be flattered but instead she was

uncomfortable. She didn't want a lot of male attention. She had wanted one male's attention, and now that she had it she didn't want to let it go.

That was her problem. Lance had moved forward and she was supposed to be, too, but if her reaction to Marcus's friendly flirting was any indication, her plan was a failure. She only had eyes for Lance.

"Kate?"

"Hmm?"

He shook his head. "Is there a man behind this change?"

"How'd you guess?"

He shrugged. "I know women."

"Do you?"

"Yes, three sisters. I was raised by wolves."

"I don't think women like to be called wolves."

"True enough, but I know that when a girl— I don't mean any offense calling you a girl—gets dolled up like you are, there's a reason for it."

"Maybe I just want a change," she said, surprised that Marcus was actually helping her to understand herself. There was something hollow about the changes she'd made.

When Lance had kissed her and held her in his

arms she'd felt like a queen. But now she was back to just feeling like Old Kate, the same way she'd felt for the last few years as Lance treated her like some kind of favored pet.

"Well, this change looks very good on you. Is the big man in?"

Kate glanced down at the phone. Lance was off of his line. And it was probably way past time for Marcus to leave her office. She hoped that she didn't have guys talking to her all day. "Yes, he is."

"I'll announce myself," Marcus said.

She nodded. Marcus usually did just that. "Thanks, Marcus."

"For what?"

"For being you," she said.

"I can be so much more if you let me," Marcus said.

"For a few weeks, right?" she asked, knowing that Marcus would be the right man for a fling but nothing more. Even if she *was* leaving the company, she didn't want to have an affair with someone who worked with Lance.

This plan—which had been concocted when she'd had two glasses of wine—now seemed... silly. She needed to just keep doing her job, find a replacement for herself and get out of Brody Oil and Gas before she hurt herself any further.

"Definitely. I'm not a forever kind of man."

"Marcus, are you here to see me?"

"Sure thing, boss man. I've got good news on the new mineral rights we purchased."

"I was hoping you'd say that," Lance said. "Go on in my office. I need a word with Kate."

Marcus winked at her and then left. Lance reached over and closed the door leading to his office.

"What do you need?" she asked. She was trying to come off cool and sophisticated, but it was really hard when she felt like she was twelve. Why had she given this man so much power over her?

"I wanted to apologize for my behavior earlier."

"I think we already covered that," Kate said. The last thing she wanted to do was rehash that kiss. For her, it had been incredible and the answer to many long fantasies about this man.

She turned away from him, but he put his hand on her chair and turned her back to face him. "I don't know why this is happening to us, Kate, but I am not going to be able to ignore it. You are—"

"Don't say anything else. You have a fiancée and I'm leaving this job."

"Why are you leaving?"

Kate looked up at him and thought about blasting him with the truth. But somehow she didn't think he'd react well if she said she was leaving because she loved him and watching him get married would be about the same as ripping her heart out of her body.

"I'm leaving because I can't work for you anymore."

That was as close to the truth as she could get. Lucky for her he seemed to accept that answer.

She spent the rest of the day doing her job and realizing that all of the men in the office were starting to notice her as a woman. It should have given her hope that she'd find another man and fall in love, but instead it just made her sad because the one man she'd changed for still seemed to be oblivious—even after he'd finally kissed her.

The Fourth of July barbecue was held at Lance's home in Somerset. He lived on acreage and had set up the party out near the lake on his property. There was an area for beach volleyball, which Lance had started playing when he was in college. Later on they would play the annual management-versus-workers match.

The caterers had been cooking since before dawn and mouthwatering smells filled the air. There was a deejay playing music under a tent near the caterers and everything had been decorated in red, white and blue.

He spotted Kate first thing as he approached the party area. "Happy Fourth of July."

"You, too. Where do you need me?"

"Well, Mitch is running late, so if you want to work here with me handing out name tags and welcoming everyone, that'd be great."

The first year they'd held the barbecue they'd started the tradition of personally welcoming everyone to the event. He, Mitch and Kate. It had been the first function where they'd really needed her.

"I can't believe this is your last year doing this," he said.

He'd given up on trying to convince her not to quit. She'd made it clear that she wasn't going to change her mind, and given that he was trying to make a go at being a decent fiancé to Lexi, he thought he should probably stop trying to convince the woman who he was having nightly fantasies about to stay on.

"Me, neither. I'm going to miss it a lot. But you'll have a new hostess for this next year."

"Yes, we will. I think Lexi is anxious to talk to you about the planning of this event so she will know what's involved."

Kate bit her lower lip but nodded. "I'll invite her to the postmortem meeting with our party-planning team. It will give her a chance to get know everyone, as well."

"Thanks. Are you staying in Somerset tonight?"

"I don't know. My folks went up to Frisco to visit my brother and his family."

"You don't see your parents much, do you?"

"We're not close," she said. "I mean, they are busy with their lives and I am busy working. But if I needed more time with them, they'd be here."

Lance had learned from his own parents that the family he could count on was the one he'd made for himself. He counted his brother and Darius as his family, and the other men who were being inducted into the Texas Cattleman's Club with him.

He'd been in touch with Darius the day before to ask him about the fire, but so far there had been little news of what was going on there.

"Have you heard from Mitch? When I talked to him yesterday he said he might be running late. But we are going to need him for the annual prize announcements."

"Yes, we will," Lance said. "Feel up to playing volleyball on my team this year?"

"Oh, I don't know."

"Every year you say you will next year. But this is your last year…."

"What good will come from me playing?" she asked. "I'm not very athletic."

"It's all for fun. Come on, Kate." He wanted to spend as much of the day with her as he could. At least until Lexi got here. He realized he had to force himself to think about Lexi. All he could think about was Kate.

"Okay, I'll play, but only if Mitch gets here so one of us can man the welcome table."

"He will be here," Lance said. "What's in the goody bag this year?"

"The T-shirt and some other company goodies. We have water guns for the kids."

"Why just the kids?" Lance asked with a grin.

"Because of last year when you and Mitch didn't know when to stop."

"Are you still upset about being caught in the cross fire?"

"Of course not," she said.

He remembered how Kate had looked with her baggy T-shirt soaking wet and clinging to her breasts. To be fair, that was when he'd noticed that there was more to his secretary than met the eye, but she'd looked so distressed by the entire thing that he'd taken his shirt off and offered it to her. She'd taken it and then left a few minutes later.

"What are you thinking?" she asked.

"About the way you looked in that wet T-shirt last year."

She flushed. "Well, don't. You're not supposed to think things like that. Remember, you said you didn't want any more temptation."

"I'm thinking that wasn't my wisest decision, Kate."

"Why not?"

He glanced around the yard quickly. It was still early so there wasn't anyone here yet except for the party crew who was setting up. He touched her face and looked down into her big brown eyes.

"I can't ignore the way you make me feel."

She bit her lower lip. "Please don't."

"Don't what? Don't want you?"

She pulled back. "Don't say things like that. Because I will believe them and do something silly like kiss you. Then you will change your mind and I'll feel stupid again."

"Don't feel stupid," Lance said. He leaned down and kissed her. He'd been wanting to for the last two days since he'd seen Marcus leaning against her desk and talking to her.

He wanted to make sure she knew that he was the only man she needed to kiss.

Her lips felt so right against his and he realized he'd been more than hungry for her. Lexi or no Lexi, was tired of denying himself Kate.

Five

Mitch arrived at the picnic looking every inch the successful lobbyist. There was a part of Lance that envied his younger brother. But with Kate at his side and now his younger brother, too, Lance felt pretty good.

"You two seem happy," Mitch said. "Did Lance finally talk you into staying on as his secretary?

Kate shook her head, and Lance realized there was still a lot of work for him to do before he had his Katie-girl back for good.

"Let's go to my office at the house and call Darius," Lance said.

"Right now?"

"Yes. I haven't had a chance to check back in with him today and the press is calling, looking for an update."

"Senator Cavanaugh is waiting for answers, as well. And until he gets them, I'm afraid that no matter what your relationship is with Lexi, he won't back the bill we need him to," Mitch said.

Lance was impressed with his younger brother. He looked nothing like their father and yet he had the old man's drive. And Mitch was savvy when it came to dealing with politicians. Lance himself was only good with gas and oil people.

"Why are you looking at me like that?" Mitch asked.

"Just wondering where you get this polish you have."

Mitch shrugged. "Mom, I guess."

"Probably. I always forget about her," Lance said. Alicia Brody had done the best she could. And when she'd walked away from their old man, Lance knew it was because she'd had enough of the roughness of her life. He'd learned a long time ago to just bury his feelings of abandonment.

"You know, I get why she left me behind," Lance said as they entered his house. "I'm the spitting image of him. But I never understood why she left you."

Mitch rubbed the back of his neck as he headed for the bar in the living room. "I think she didn't want either of us to be alone. I've always imagined she knew that if I didn't stay she'd lose you, too."

Lance didn't like the sound of that. He'd always thought of himself as the protector, the one who'd kept Mitch safe. "Really?"

"Hell, I don't know. I'm not a woman and to be fair, I don't understand them," Mitch said.

Lance laughed. His own situation with women was beyond complicated at the moment. Getting engaged hadn't made his life any easier like he'd imagined it would. Although he'd resolved to be the man Lexi deserved, he just couldn't keep his lips off Kate.

"Speaking of women, I got Lexi a necklace. Do you think she's the type of woman who'd enjoy receiving it in public?" Lance asked.

Mitch poured two fingers of whiskey into a

highball glass and downed it in one swallow. "No."

"I wasn't sure. I guess I'll give it to her when she shows up at the house later. I'm glad she's coming today."

"Her dad asked her to. I believe he wants to know what we are like beyond the glitter of DC."

"Cavanaugh knows what we are like. Texans, like him. And he shouldn't forget that."

Mitch poured some whiskey for Lance and held the glass out to him.

"To Texas boys."

Lance clinked his glass against his brother's and downed his whiskey in a quick swallow. He liked the burn as it went down.

The band started playing out back. "Let's get this business with Darius wrapped up so we can enjoy the party."

"Good idea."

Lance led the way down the hall to his den. It was decorated in dark hues of brown and leather. He'd picked out the furniture for this room himself instead of leaving it to the interior designer. He'd known exactly how he wanted the room to look.

There was a Remington black and white photograph on the wall, and a portrait painting of

Mitch and him that had been done when their first well came in. In the background was Old Tilly, as they liked to call her.

"Remember that day?" Mitch asked.

"Hell, yes. I think about it often. It was when I knew you and I were going to make it."

"I always knew we would," Mitch said. "Neither of us knows how to quit."

"True that." Lance dialed the speakerphone and Darius answered on the second ring.

"Darius here."

"It's Lance and Mitch,"

"Happy Fourth. I suppose you are calling about your arson investigation," Darius said.

Lance liked that Darius was straight to the point. He was one of Lance's best friends and the kind of guy that Lance knew he could count on.

"We are."

"I'm afraid I don't have much news. They are still saying arson and they found the source that started the fire but now they have to eliminate several possibilities as accelerants. Once they find the one used at your blaze, they will start investigating where the accelerant was sold."

"How long do you think that will take?" Lance asked.

"Who knows? But I'm in touch with them every day and you can take my word that they are working hard on your case."

Darius gave them a few more details and he and Lance made plans for drinks later in the week before hanging up.

"Are you going to be in town next week?"

"If I get Senator Cavanaugh back on our side. If not, I think I should stay in DC. This is a critical time in our dealings with him."

Lance nodded. "Thank you for doing this."

"It's my company, too, and I want it to succeed as badly as you do," Mitch said.

Lance believed that. When the old man had died, they'd both taken a vow to put the company first and make it the best damned oil and gas company in the world.

They'd had some ups and downs with hurricanes and workers' strikes, but together he and Mitch had conquered everything that came their way. This arson issue was just a complication—nothing the two of them couldn't handle.

Kate tried not to think too much about the kiss that Lance had given her at the sign-in table. She just kept her sunglasses on and her head down as she stood in the sand, playing—of all things—beach volleyball.

Lance was serving and he was very good at it. But then he was good at everything he did. And he was built for sports. Though most of the men who worked for Brody Oil and Gas were in shape, no one looked better to her than Lance Brody. She remembered last year when he'd taken his shirt off to give it to her.

He was built like an Ultimate Fighting Championship fighter and from what she had heard of his past, he'd grown up hard with a father who liked to fight.

"Kate!"

She turned around to face the net just as the ball came toward her. She lifted her hands not to hit the ball but to protect her head. She really hated playing these kind of games.

The ball bounced off her, heading toward the ground, when Marcus dove to the sand to hit it up. Joan took the ball and spiked it over the net.

Kate was shaken by her near miss and decided it was time for her to stop playing. "I'm going to sit out."

No one objected and she felt good about that. She sat on the sidelines where she watched the rest of the game and she talked to some of the families of workers who'd been with Brody Oil and Gas since Mitch and Lance had taken over after their father's death.

A lot of people commented on her new look, telling her how nice it was. She thanked them. She was starting to get used to how she looked and no longer saw a stranger in the mirror.

She grabbed a bottle of water as the game ended with Lance's team victorious. She handed the water to him and he hugged her close. "We won."

"As usual," she said, with a smile. This was one thing she'd really miss about Lance. When they were at his house, she never felt like his secretary.

"Winning is what I do best," Lance said.

"Very true," she said, thinking that was probably one of the things that drew her to him. He just had a positive attitude and kept on going until he achieved what he set out for.

"Walk with me up toward the house."

"Why?"

"Because I want to talk to you. Do you have all the fireworks set up for us?"

"Yes. Exactly as they were last year. I have the music cued and the deejay is ready to announce everything for you."

Everyone wanted to talk to Lance and though he had asked her to stay with him, she soon found herself drifting to the outside of his circle. It was then that she spotted Mitch at the welcome table with Lexi Cavanaugh.

The woman was beautiful and sophisticated and everything that Kate wasn't. She'd be the perfect match for Lance—being a senator's daughter, she knew how to socialize and work in the community. Brody Oil and Gas was always looking for ways to give back to the communities where their refineries were. And Lexi would be a conduit to that.

"Join me for a beer?"

Kate glanced over at Marcus. He had two Bud Lights and held one of them out to her. She smiled and took it. "Thanks for saving me from that ball earlier."

"No problem. You definitely looked like you were out of your league."

She shrugged. "I figured I should play at least one time before leaving."

"So the rumors are true," Marcus said. He tipped his bottle back and took a long swallow of his beer.

He was an attractive man, she realized. He

was tall, at least six foot five, and had a neatly trimmed red beard. His hair was longish on the top but cut neat in the back.

"Yes, they are true," she said, sipping her beer.

"I think it's safe to say we are all going to miss you," Marcus said.

"I doubt it. There will be someone else in Lance's office keeping you guys all organized."

"But that person won't be you," Marcus said.

"I'd take that to heart but you didn't even notice me until I had my makeover," she said, looking at him closely. As attractive as Marcus might be, he didn't hold a candle to Lance.

"True enough. But that doesn't mean I'm not telling the truth now."

"Can I ask you something?"

"Sure," Marcus said.

"Why was I invisible before?" she asked. "It was more than clothes and glasses, right?"

Marcus took another swallow of his beer. "It was more than that. I think it was your attitude. You weren't invisible exactly, I'd say you were more of the girl next door, you know? Just a comfortable woman who we didn't see as a sexual being."

"But now you do?"

"Yes, now I do. I can't speak for anyone else."

Kate nodded looked away

"I'm not the man you wanted to notice you, right?"

She shook her head. "You're a good-looking guy but not the one for me."

He threw his head back and laughed. "Well, there is justice in the universe. I can't tell you how many times I've used almost that exact line."

That made Kate laugh. She gave Marcus a quick kiss on the cheek before turning to walk away. And she stepped right into Lance who had been standing behind her.

Lance took Kate's arm and led her away from Marcus. He'd never felt so enraged before. He wanted to be the man who made her laugh and smile—not Marcus.

"Are you okay?" Kate asked.

"I…no, I'm not okay. I don't like you flirting with Marcus."

"Why do you care who I flirt with?" Kate said, a flash of anger in her eyes.

Because she was his. But he knew that wasn't true, couldn't be true because he'd given another woman his ring.

A woman that he was quickly realizing he could never marry. Lexi was not what he needed in a woman. She didn't arouse his passion. But passion could lead to jealousy and Lance couldn't afford to be out of control, to be like his father. Maybe that was the right answer, then. Maybe Kate would be better off with a guy like Marcus, and he should marry someone who didn't get him all riled.

"Damn. I know I don't have any right to say something like that, but I want you, Kate. And I think you feel the same," he said.

She flushed but didn't try to pull away. "I do. I think you should know I've been attracted to you for the longest time."

"Good."

"Good?" she asked. "That makes you sound very arrogant."

"Yes, it is good," Lance said. He'd had a lot of time to think about Kate over the last two days. "Because anything this strong that is one-sided would be wrong."

"I guess I can see your point."

"I'm glad," he said. He leaned down and kissed her. "Come up to the house with me while I shower and change."

"Into the shower with you?" she asked.

He raised both eyebrows at her. "Would you be interested in that?"

She blushed and gave him a very shy smile. "Maybe."

He was leading her by the hand toward the house when he saw paramedics running across the lawn. He dropped Kate's hand and they both turned toward the food tent.

"I have to see who that is," he said.

"I know."

He was very aware of Kate moving behind him and he knew that she was concerned about the emergency, the same as he was.

Lexi was sitting on a bench between two paramedics. Her face was flushed.

"What happened?"

"Heat exhaustion as near as we can tell," the paramedic said.

"Are you okay?" Lance asked Lexi.

She nodded, seeming embarrassed by the entire thing. "I should have had more water."

"It's okay. Does she need to go to the emergency room?" Lance asked.

"No. She'd be fine sitting in a cool room and just letting her body recuperate from the sun exposure."

"Let's get you up to the house," Lance said.

Kate hovered nearby. The look on her face told Lance that it was past time to end things with Lexi. But not now. Not like this.

He helped Lexi to her feet. She leaned on him and he looked over her head at Kate who shook her head and walked away.

He had no choice but to let her leave and he didn't like that at all. But right now his hands were tied. He couldn't go after Kate until he took care of Lexi.

He got Lexi settled on the couch in the living room.

"Thank you, Lance."

"For what?" he asked. He hardly knew Lexi. She was a stunningly beautiful woman but other than a couple of dinners, he hadn't really even talked to her.

"For taking care of me just now. I'm sorry if that was embarrassing."

Lance shrugged. "It was nothing. I'm going to go change. Will you be okay?"

She nodded.

"I have a butler of sorts around here—Paul. He's not much company but I will ask him to check in on you."

She shook her head. "Please don't. I'll just sit here in the quiet."

"Are you sure?"

"Yes."

Lance left her and walked up the stairs to his own suite. He called Mitch on his way because he hadn't been able to find his brother in the crowded yard.

"Brody here."

"It's Lance. Can you come up to the house? Lexi had a problem with heat exhaustion. I need a shower but I don't want to leave her alone for too long."

"Is she okay?" Mitch asked.

"Pale and weak but otherwise okay," Lance said.

"Does she need to see a doctor?"

"No. The paramedics checked her out. Where were you?"

Mitch didn't answer. "I'm on my way to the house."

"Good. I'm upstairs. She didn't seem to want company but I don't like leaving her alone when she's not at her best."

"I agree. I'll take care of it."

Lance hung up and quickly showered and

changed. He thought about the two women that were a part of his life right now. It didn't matter that Lexi wasn't the woman he wanted, he still owed her respect—and the truth.

He realized this mess was of his own making. He finished getting dressed and headed downstairs, determined to talk to Lexi. He couldn't marry her—not while he felt what he did for Kate.

Kate was the woman he couldn't live without. He knew without a doubt that Kate was the one woman that he wanted. He couldn't get her out of his system.

He hurried downstairs, anxious to talk to his brother and fiancée. He had a text message from Mitch saying that he was going to take Lexi to the hotel.

Having made up his mind about Lexi and Kate, Lance felt much better. He liked the changes in his plain-Jane secretary and today he'd realized that he wasn't going to let her slip away from him—no matter what.

Six

Lexi Cavanauagh was a stunningly gorgeous woman by anyone's standards. The fact that she was his fiancée should have made him feel lucky. But she was essentially a stranger and he felt awkward around her. Not at all like he felt with Kate.

Kate. He'd already decided to end things with Lexi. But he had to be careful. He needed Lexi and her connections but he couldn't just break things off with her.

Lance came back down the stairs to the sound of raised voices. "Everything okay?"

Mitch and Lexi were standing across the room from each other. Lexi's fists were clenched at her sides and a sheen of tears glittered in her eyes.

"Lexi, what's the matter?"

"Nothing," she said.

"Mitch?"

"We were discussing an event we attended in D.C.," Mitch said.

Lance nodded. "I'm glad to see you feeling better, Lexi. I wanted to take a moment to welcome you to the family. You already know Mitch and I think you will see that we are a close group despite there being only two of us."

"I have noticed that your brother will do anything for you," Lexi said.

Mitch gave her a tense look.

"And I for him."

Lance walked across the room to the foyer where he'd left the neatly wrapped gift box. It bore the emblem of his favorite jeweler and a discreet white bow. He carried it back over and smiled at Lexi.

She didn't seem to be paying any attention to him. "Do you need to sit down?"

"No. I need to go home," she said.

"Then I will take you," Lance said.

She shook her head and noticed the box in his hands. "Is that for me?"

"Yes," he said, handing it to her.

She took it. He noticed that her nails were long and manicured. And for the first time he tried to imagine what it would be like to take Lexi to his bed. He couldn't. The only woman he pictured there was Kate.

Kate's long brown hair on his pillow. Kate's pretty brown eyes staring up at him…Kate was the woman he wanted.

Lexi sat down and opened the gift box carefully. Lance stood across the room with the first niggling of doubt since he'd asked her to marry him. Had he made a colossal mistake?

She held the box in her hands, not opening it. "Why did you get me a gift?"

"To thank you for agreeing to be my wife."

She put her head down and opened the box. He heard her breath catch and took that as a good sign.

He glanced over at his brother and Mitch stared at Lexi…the way Lance realized he stared at Kate sometimes. Damn, was his brother into Lexi?

"Will you help me put it on?" Lexi asked.

Lance started toward her and saw Mitch do the same.

His brother shrugged. "I'm just used to filling in for you."

"Thank you for that, Mitch. Without your help, I don't know what I would have done."

Lexi stood up and lifted her hair. Lance fastened the diamond necklace around her neck.

"Yes, thanks, Mitch, for filling in for your brother so well," Lexi said.

"It was no big deal. I'm used to dealing with problematic heiresses."

"Are you?" Lexi asked.

"Indeed. Our mother was one."

"She sure was. But Lexi isn't anything like Mom," Lance said, not sure what was going on between his brother and Lexi.

"No, she's not," Mitch said. Mitch's cell phone rang and he excused himself to take the call.

Lance found himself alone with his fiancée for the first time since she'd agreed to marry him. And he needed to know if there was any chance this relationship was going to work between them. He put his hands on her shoulders and turned her in his arms.

She looked up at him. Her eyes wide but not with passion, more with…he couldn't identify the emotion.

He brushed a kiss against her lips and found that her mouth was dry and the kiss was rather blah.

Lance worried that he'd be trapped in a passionless marriage. It was clear that Lexi wasn't attracted to him and he knew he wasn't to her.

"Thank you for the gift. It's very pretty."

"You're welcome," he said.

A horn honked outside and Lexi glanced at her watch. "That should be my cab."

"I would've taken you," Lance said.

"I didn't want to be a bother. Thank you for inviting me to the party today. I really enjoyed the chance to see what kind of a company Brody Oil & Gas is."

"You're welcome. Kate said she was going to invite you to attend a meeting with the party-planning staff."

"Sounds great. I'll look forward to her call," Lexi said as she left the house and walked to her cab. She kept talking brightly the entire time and Lance held the door for her as she got into the cab.

She smiled up at him as she said goodbye and he closed the door, standing there watching her be driven away.

He rubbbed the back of his neck, having a bad feeling that his marriage to Lexi was going to be a mistake. And he prided himself on not making any mistakes. He wondered if he should have ended things with her today, but he couldn't have. There was something vulnerable about Lexi. He needed to talk to Mitch about his feelings for her, as well.

There was more between the two of them than he could guess at. But that was a worry for another day. Right now he had a party to host and several staff members to take care of and that was exactly what he was going to do.

After he found Kate.

He needed to talk to her and see her. She had always been his touchstone at Brody Oil & Gas and he realized he needed her by his side now.

Kate was glad when the sun set. Soon it would be time for the Fourth of July fireworks to go off. They had always been her favourite. She'd spent most of the afternoon and evening trying to avoid Lance.

She felt…well, stupid. She was supposed to be getting over him, not falling deeper in love with him each day.

It was silly, really, but seeing the way he'd reacted to Lexi's being sick had affected her. For all his rough ways, she knew that Lance was the kind of guy who'd stand by his friends, no matter what.

And there had been a part of her that had realized that he treated Lexi like a friend and nothing more. Much the same way he'd been treating her for all these years until she'd quit.

What Kate needed was another job in another town, but she really couldn't imagine living anywhere other than south Texas. Unlike some of her friends from high school, she'd never wanted to live anywhere except here.

She liked the warmth and humidity that came with Houston. She liked the cosmopolitan city aspects of the area and the wide-open spaces that were only a few hours' drive away.

A few kids were running around with sparklers and Kate felt a lump at the back of her throat as she thought about the families.

She'd always wanted one of her own but it had never really seemed like she'd have one and now…well, now she seemed no closer to having kids and a husband than she'd been for a while.

"Hey, girl!" Becca called.

"Becca! I'm so glad you could swing by here. Thanks for coming." Kate gave her friend a hug and they walked up the tiki-light path toward the viewing area for the fireworks.

"Wouldn't have missed it for the world. Sorry it took so long to get here."

"Not a problem," Kate said. "I think Lance is going to the Texas Cattleman's Club later for an after-party and I just wanted…"

"A friend," Becca said. "I get it. So how was everything today?"

"Well, good, I think. I kissed Lance and it was…"

"What?"

"Everything I imagined it would be. But then Lexi had heat exhaustion and he had to go to her."

Becca slipped her arm through Kate's. "Was she okay?"

"Yes. But it made me realize I don't want to have an affair with Lance. I want to be able to have a relationship with him where we can be seen as a couple. Not one where I have to hide."

"Good for you. Being a mistress isn't something that would suit you," Becca said.

"Would it suit you?"

"Hell, no."

Both women laughed.

"Is there any other man you are interested in?" Becca asked.

"Not really. I think that Marcus likes me."

Becca laughed again, and Kate relaxed for the first time all day, feeling safe in the presence of her friend. Becca was the one person who she knew loved her no matter what. She didn't care if Kate was fat or wore ugly clothes—Becca liked her anyway.

"That's not surprising, you're a very attractive woman."

"Yeah, right. You're my friend, you have to say that," Kate said. "One thing that was shocking was Lance. He didn't like me flirting with Marcus."

"Too bad," Becca said. "Lance Brody had his chance with you and he let it slip by."

"Maybe I regret that, Becca."

"Good," Becca said. "It's about time you realized that, Lance."

Kate flushed with embarrassment as Lance stepped up behind them.

"Yes, it is," Lance said.

Lance joined the women and they went to the main BBQ area. They chatted while the band played, and Becca got up to dance. Kate glanced at Lance. She felt like she wanted to dance, too, but knew they couldn't—not while he was engaged to Lexi.

"I have something I want to show you," Lance said, and led her away from the crowd.

"The perfect spot to watch the fireworks."

"Where would that be?"

"In my arms."

She stopped. "Don't say anything you don't mean, Lance."

"I'm not."

"What about Lexi? How is she, by the way?" Kate asked. What she'd seen of the Senator's daughter had been brief, but she bore the woman no ill will.

"Fine. She went back to her hotel to get some rest."

"That's good," Kate said. "I can't do this—have an affair with a man who belongs to another woman."

Lance cupped her face in his hands. "Today cemented for me the fact that I need you, Kate.

I'm sorry I didn't wake up earlier to the fact that you are an incredible woman."

Kate steeled her heart against just believing his words. "What changed your mind?"

"Seeing your hot body," he said.

"That's not flattering," she said.

"Yes, it is. And it's the truth. I'm not going to lie to you and try to make you believe that I had some kind of emotional realization when you said you were going to quit. It was really when I got a look at you…I realized that you had everything I wanted."

"Lance—"

"What? Would you prefer I made up lies and told you stories? You know I'm not that kind of guy. I'm also not the kind of man who lets something he wants slip through his fingers. And I want you, Kate."

His raw language got to her as little else could. She'd long wanted Lance and hearing him tell her that he felt the same…it was a powerful aphrodisiac.

He pulled her into his arms and kissed her. There was a lot of passion in his kiss and she stopped trying to think this through, stopped trying to make her attraction to Lance go away.

The thought that maybe this was the only way to free herself entered her mind.

But she knew she was only placating herself. She wanted Lance Brody and now that he had his arms around her, she wasn't going to walk away. Not until she had the chance to experience what it was really like to be his woman.

That was the one thing she'd wanted since her very first day at Brody Oil and Gas. She wrapped her arms around his shoulders and went up on tiptoe to bring her body more fully into contact with his.

He slid his tongue over hers and she tangled her fingers in the silky hair at the back of his neck. As she ran her fingers through it, she felt everything inside of her clench.

She was in Lance's arms!

Lance had no real plan of seduction. He just wanted to kiss Kate because it seemed a sacrilege not to. This was the Fourth of July and he was a red-blooded male, a Texan who'd learned the hard way that you had to fight for what you wanted.

And he wanted Kate Thornton. He lifted her into his arms and stepped off the lighted path. He walked up to his house with patriotic music blaring in the background and fireworks going off all around them.

Kate rested her head on his shoulder and held on to him with a strong grip. He knew that the attraction between them was mutual but until this moment hadn't realized just how much that would mean to him.

He just wanted to know what she'd be like in his bed. To know if the woman he couldn't live without in his work life would also be as important to his personal life. His gut said yes.

"You look fierce," she said.

"Do I?"

She nodded. "Are you sure about this?"

"Hell yes," he said, reaching down to open the door to the living room. He walked up the stairs to his bedroom without pausing to turn on a light.

"I'm not," she said.

The shyness in her voice stopped him. He couldn't force himself on her. He never wanted passion between them to be all about him. He knew Kate well enough, had observed the changes in her and knew she had doubts about herself.

And he wanted to show her that he loved her as she was…well, loved her body, he corrected.

"I'm not rushing you, Kate," Lance said. He set her on her feet and led her out onto his private balcony, gesturing to one of the lounge chairs that faced the east and the fireworks.

"How about a red-hot and boom?"

She shook her head. "I had one last year and think I still might be a little drunk from it."

He laughed. It was then that he realized he was nervous. He knew his way around an oil field and a boardroom but a woman—one who mattered to him—that was an entirely different subject. And Kate had somehow become this woman who mattered to him.

"Champagne?" he asked.

"I'm good," she said.

"Still nervous?"

"A little. You know, I've been wanting to be here with you…like this…for longer than I can remember," she said.

"Is it what you imagined?"

She shook her head, those long silky curls of hers brushing against her collar.

"What can I do to make it better?" he asked. He sat down next to her and put his arm around her shoulder. She was practically a little bird now with tiny arms and shoulders. He hugged her close. "Why'd you lose weight?"

She shrugged and looked away.

"Sorry, was that too personal?"

She started to nod and then turned to pin him with her dark-chocolate stare. "I had to. It wasn't healthy for me and I was tired of being invisible."

"You weren't completely," he said.

"Yes, I was. Or you would have invited me up here a lot sooner," she said, standing up.

She paced over to the railing and leaned back against it, facing him.

"Does it bother you that I didn't?"

"Of course. But not for the reasons you think. It bothers me because I have wasted so many years of my life."

"You're not old, Kate," he said.

"I'm old enough. And it took your engagement to another woman to snap me out of the trance I've been in."

"My engagement?"

"I told you, I've wanted you for a long time," Kate said.

"I'm sorry, Katie-girl. My engagement…it was done for political purposes."

"Really? What about Lexi? Does she know that? Don't you care for her at all?"

Lance stood up, as well. "She knows that we are engaged for our families' sakes. And to be honest, tonight I realized that I can't go through with the fake engagement."

"Why not?"

Lance wasn't the kind of man who liked to talk about his feelings but he knew better than to keep quiet this time. "It just didn't seem right to marry her."

He walked slowly over to Kate, stopping when barely an inch of space separated them. "Don't you want to know why?"

Kate stared up at him. How could he have ever missed how beautiful her eyes were?

"Why?" she asked in a breathy voice.

"I can't marry her when you are the one woman I can't get out of my mind."

"You can't… Are you serious?"

"Serious as a heart attack, baby. And I'm not about to let you go until we've figured this out."

Seven

Kate felt overwhelmed by Lance. She put her hands on his chest and leaned forward to kiss him, licking her lips the second before her mouth touched his. She kept her mouth open, feeling the exhalation of his breath against her. She closed her eyes and rubbed her lips over his.

She let herself make this moment into a memory that she'd remember for the rest of her life. If the last week had taught her anything it was that Lance was important to her. And that forever… well, forever might not be in the cards for them.

But now was. Right now. She curled her fingers around his arms and touched his tongue lightly with hers, stroking it into his open mouth. She tasted the beer he'd drunk earlier and something that was starting to be familiar to her. A taste that was just Lance.

She started to withdraw from his mouth and felt his teeth close lightly around her tongue. He angled his head and she felt his hand on her ribs right below her breasts. His other hand tangled in the hair at the back of her head.

He held her so strongly as his mouth moved over hers, as he took complete control of the embrace and of her body. Shivers spread down her body from her lips past her neck. Her breasts felt fuller as she continued kissing him. She leaned forward and felt the tips of her breasts brush his chest.

She moaned, and then was embarrassed and broke away.

He stopped her. "What is it, honey?"

She shook her head. How had she thought that she could be with this sophisticated man? Had she forgotten that the hair and clothes were just window dressing? Inside she was still Kate Thornton.

But this was Lance Brody and he didn't take

no for an answer. He pulled her back into his arms, his hands falling to the small of her back, holding her against his rock-hard body. His erection nudged the bottom of her stomach.

She glanced up and saw that he was watching her. And she realized she wanted to see more of him. All of him. How often did dreams come true?

If she walked away now, the makeover would be just what she'd called it—window dressing. Nothing more than a facade on her dusty old life. But she had changed.

She put her hands on Lance's face, drew his head down to hers. "You are the best kisser."

He smiled at her, just a little half smile that made her pulse race. "I'm just getting started."

Kate let herself relax and stop worrying about the future, about everything other than this moment. She wanted Lance. He wanted her. Together, they were going to make this moment one of the most memorable.

Lance kissed her again and then lifted her in his arms. She realized she liked the way he carried her around. She loved the feeling that came with being in his arms. Since Kate was big for most of her life, Lance was the first man to carry her as an adult. And it made her feel beautiful, like the sexy girls that men always carried in the movies.

Lance carried her over the threshold, back into his bedroom. He kissed her so tenderly before slowly undressing her.

She crossed her arms over her breasts, knowing despite the weight loss that she still wasn't perfect. This body…she glanced down at it. Her breasts had fine white stretch marks. And her stomach wasn't flat. She wondered sometimes if it would ever be.

"What are you doing?"

"I'm not very good-looking naked," she said.

He shook his head and drew her hands away from her body, holding her arms open so she felt so damned exposed. Too exposed. She couldn't do this.

Just when she was about to turn away, he pulled her into his arms, hugging her close to his clothed body. "Kate, can't you feel what you do to me?"

He took her hand and drew it down his body to his erection. It was hard and proud, pressing against his jeans. She stroked him through his clothes.

He traced his finger over her breasts, circling around the white fleshy globe before coming closer to her nipple. It beaded up and she bit her lower lip, waiting in anticipation of his touch.

"Katie?"

"Hmm?"

"You have one hot, sexy body," he said. His finger rubbed over her nipple, making it impossible for her to remember her own arguments.

A moment later, his head dipped down and he suckled her, drawing her nipple into his mouth. She rubbed her hands over his short hair.

"Lance, take your shirt off," she said. She surprised herself with her demand. But she wanted to enjoy every second she had with Lance, and she *needed* to see his chest.

He lifted his head and stood there in front of her. "You take it off for me."

She reached for his shirt and drew it up and over his head. He tossed it aside and she couldn't help but reach for his chest. She touched his muscles over his breastbone and then followed the line of hair that tapered down, disappearing into his waistband.

"I like you without your shirt on," she said.

"Do you?"

"Yes."

She felt more vulnerable now than she had just a second before. She hadn't meant to leave herself so open to him. Yet, at the same time, she knew there was no other way for her to react to him.

He didn't say anything else, just bent to trace the line of her neck to the base. He licked her there and then dropped the softest kiss on her.

She couldn't think as he stood back up and lifted her onto the bed. He bent down to capture the tip of her breast in his mouth. He sucked her deep in his mouth, his teeth lightly scraping against her sensitive flesh. His other hand played at her other breast, arousing her, making her arch against him in need.

She fumbled with his trousers. He should be naked. She pulled back. Again the brazen woman she hadn't realized she was came to the scene. "Take your pants off."

He stood up and unfastened them, kicking off his pants and underwear in one smooth move. He came back down on top of her. She reached between them and took his erection in her hand, bringing him closer to her, spreading her legs wider so that she was totally open to him. "I need you now."

He lifted his head; the tips of her breasts were damp from his mouth and very tight. He rubbed his chest over them. Then he donned a condom.

She slid her hands down his back, cupping his butt as he thrust into her loosely. Their eyes met. Staring deep into his eyes made her feel like their souls were meeting. She felt her body start to tighten around him, catching her by surprise. She climaxed before him. He gripped her hips, holding her down and thrusting into her two more times before he came with a loud grunt of her name.

After disposing of the condom, he held her, pulling her into his arms and tucking her up against his side.

She wrapped her arm around him and listened to the solid beating of his heart. She closed her eyes and let out her breath, snuggling closer to this man that she'd wanted and loved for so long. She felt his arms wrap around her and she realized that in this moment, she had everything she'd ever wanted. Her dreams were coming true.

Lance woke up with a hard-on and his hands on Kate's breasts. She felt so incredibly good. He rubbed his erection against her buttocks and lowered his head to her neck. She shifted in his arms, rubbing against him.

He nibbled on the skin exposed by the morning sunlight. She was beautiful. He knew she didn't think so but as he looked down her body, wrapped in his arms, he'd never seen a more beautiful woman.

He rubbed his palm over her breast until her eyes opened halfway and she moaned softly. The same noise she'd made last night when he'd made love to her.

He shifted on the bed, so that he was lying next to her, his morning hard-on pressing against her hip. It had been a long time since he'd had a woman sleep over and it felt right to Lance that Kate was there.

"Morning." He took her mouth with his, letting his hands wander over her body. That she was here in his bedroom was just as it should be.

"Good morning," she said, putting her hand in front of her mouth.

He pulled her hand away from her face and kissed her. "You taste good this morning, honey." He swept his hand down her body. "Look good, too."

She flushed and buried her red face against his chest. He put his arms around her and held her. He didn't understand it but Kate was more beautiful this morning than she had been last night. Her dark hair was thick and curled in disarray around her shoulders. The makeup she'd had on yesterday had worn off and her eyes were clear.

"You slept with your contacts in. Do you need to take them out?"

She shook her head. "I got the kind you can wear for a month. I had a really hard time getting them in initially."

"Then why wear them?"

"Glasses were part of the old me."

"So was I, but not anymore."

Kate laughed. "Glasses have always been a mask for me to hide behind and I don't want to do that anymore."

He traced his hand over her shoulder and down her back. She shivered with awareness and her nipples beaded. She was so wonderfully responsive. He pushed her back down on the bed and then bent to lick each nipple. He blew gently on the tips. She raked her nails down his back.

"What are you doing?" she asked.

"Making love to you this morning," he answered, kissing his way to her stomach and tasting her flesh there.

"Why?"

"Because I can," he said.

He kissed her soundly, thrusting his tongue deep into her mouth until she was writhing on the bed and moaning his name.

He continued to kiss and nibble his way down her body, taking time to draw her nipples out by suckling them. When she arched off the bed and clutched his head to her breasts, he decided to move lower, to nibble at her stomach and trace the faint scars left from her weight loss. He hadn't realized how proud he was of Kate until now. She'd really taken charge of her life.

He moved lower until he knelt between her thighs and looked down at her. "May I kiss you there?"

She swallowed, her hands shifting on the bed next to her hips.

"No one has ever done that," she said.

"If you don't like it, I'll stop," he said.

Her legs moved and he took that as a yes.

He leaned down, blowing lightly on her before tonguing her soft flesh. She lifted her hips toward his mouth.

He wrapped his hands around her hips and drew her up to him, holding her to his mouth as he tasted her. He pushed her legs farther apart until he could reach her dewy core. He pushed his finger into her body and drew out some of her moisture; he lifted his head and looked up her body.

Her eyes were closed, her head tipped back, her shoulders arched, throwing her breasts forward with their berry-hard tips, begging for more attention. Her entire body was erotically beautiful in the morning sunlight.

He lowered his head again, hungry for more of her. He feasted on her body, carefully tasting the moist flesh between her legs. He used his teeth, tongue and fingers to bring her to the brink of climax but held her there, wanting to draw out the moment of completion until she was begging him for it.

Her hands grasped his head as she thrust her hips up toward his face. But he pulled back so that she didn't get the contact she craved.

"Lance, please."

He scraped his teeth over her clitoris and she screamed as her orgasm rocked through her body. He kept his mouth on her until her body stopped shuddering and then slid up her, holding her tightly in his arms.

He rolled over, keeping her with him until she straddled him. "Sit up, honey."

She did as he asked, bracing herself on his shoulders. He shifted his hips until the tip of his cock found the portal of her body. The warmth of her against him made him realize he wasn't wearing a condom. He reached for the one he'd left on the nightstand last night.

He quickly opened it. "Sit up."

"Let me do it," she said.

He handed the condom to her and with a little help from him, he was sheathed. He shifted his hips again and slipped the tip of his erection into her.

"Take as much of me as you want," he said.

"I want it all," Kate said. "But I'm not sure…"

He put his hands on her hips and guided her down on him. But the feel of her around him quickly eroded his self-control and he found himself holding her hips tightly while he thrust up inside of her, trying to get deeper. He pulled her legs forward, forcing them farther apart until she settled even closer to him.

He slid deeper still into her. She arched her back, reaching up to entwine her arms around his shoulders. He thrust harder and felt every nerve in his body tensing. Reaching between their bodies, he touched her between her legs until he felt her body start to tighten around him.

He came in a rush, continuing to thrust into her until his body was drained. He then collapsed on top of her, lying his head between her breasts.

A week later, Lance still hadn't had the chance to talk to Lexi, who had gone back to DC. But he had managed to keep Kate on as his assistant. And he'd taken her to dinner every night—and made love to her most of those nights, as well.

The investigation into the fire was going painfully slowly. Mitch was back in DC and Lance hadn't spoken to him since the Fourth. They were ready to get back to work at the main refinery. They needed to be producing barrels of oil each day, not sitting idle.

He picked up the phone and dialed Darius's number.

"This is Darius."

"Darius, my man, what news do you have from the refinery?"

"Not much. The arson investigator is still tracking the accelerant to try to find the source."

"Do you trust the man?" Lance asked. "Is he competent?"

"Yes, I think he is. I'm going to call his office later. I'll follow up with you when I have news."

"Thanks, Darius. I appreciate you taking this case."

"That's what friends are for, right?"

"Indeed."

"Speaking of friends…what's this I hear about your engagement?"

Lance looked at the open door leading to Kate's desk. He could hear her hands moving over the keyboard of her computer.

"It's complicated."

"With women, that's the only way a situation can be."

Lance laughed. "More so than usual. I can't say any more until I talk to the lady involved."

"Gotcha. I can appreciate that."

"Thanks, Darius."

He hung up the phone as Kate entered his office. "Marcus needs five minutes to talk to you later."

"Anything else?" Lance asked. Marcus was hanging around the office too much lately and Lance knew it was because of Kate.

"This came for you via courier. Said it was

urgent," she said, handing him a letter-sized envelope.

He stopped her with a hand on her wrist. He suspected the envelope held the bracelet he'd ordered for her last night. He wanted Kate to have something, and until he could talk to Lexi, a ring was out of the question.

Was he really thinking of marrying Kate Thornton?

"Close the door for me."

"No. People will talk if we close the door. It's never closed when I'm in here."

"Katie-girl…what are you thinking?"

She blushed and gave him a hard stare. "Nothing."

She turned on her heel to leave. He stopped her, reaching over her head to close the door, trapping her.

"Turn around."

She did, slowly.

"Was that so hard?"

She shook her head. "You are way too bossy for your own good."

"You like it," he said, thinking of last night when he'd ordered her to come while they were making love, and she had.

She blushed.

"What did you want from me?"

Everything, he thought. He wanted every secret in her dark brown stare to be revealed to him.

"I think this package is actually for you. Have a seat in my chair."

"Lance…"

He gestured to his chair and then followed her back across his office. She wore a short skirt and a sleeveless sweater today. Her hair had been left loose and hung down her back in silky waves.

Each day, instead of growing used to her look he found something new about her that attracted him.

He wondered if that would stop or go away with familiarity. But somehow he doubted that it would. There was something about Kate that just kept deepening for him each day.

"Why are you staring at me like that?" she asked.

He shrugged. "Just thinking about how pretty you are."

"I'm not," she said.

"That's not the way to take a compliment."

She swallowed. "But I look in the mirror every day, Lance."

He walked over to her, leaning one hip on the side of the desk. He turned her toward him and looked down into her face.

"You are beautiful, Kate. I'm not sure why I never noticed it before but you get prettier each and every day."

"Thank you, Lance. When I'm with you I feel…like the woman I always dreamed of being."

"I'm glad," he said. He reached for the envelope and checked the return address. It was the bracelet he'd ordered. He opened the envelope and a small black jewelry bag fell out.

"I'm not much of a gift wrapper, but I wanted you to have this," Lance said.

Kate reached for it and he opened the bag. He took her hand in his and turned it palm up.

He shook the jewelry bag until the bracelet dropped out into her hand. The jewel-encrusted charms glittered. She bit her lower lip and closed her fist over the bracelet.

"Thank you. It's so beautiful. But why are you giving me this?."

"I wanted you to have a piece of jewelry that

you didn't buy for yourself, something that would remind you of me each time you put it on."

The look on her face told him everything he needed to know.

Eight

Kate spent the rest of the day admiring her bracelet and romanticizing her relationship with Lance. It had developed into something altogether different than she'd expected, something more than she'd ever expected from any relationship.

She found herself cautioning her heart not to believe that Lance was the man of her dreams. She felt like there was still something that had to be worked out between them. She hadn't asked about his engagement to Lexi and if he'd broken it off. But Lance had said he would do it and she trusted him.

And the bracelet. She stopped working at her computer and touched it. It was a beautiful piece of jewelry. The only other man to ever give her any jewelry had been her dad, who had gifted her with one-karat diamond stud earrings when she'd graduated from high school.

This was different. Although her head was telling her to be cautious, her heart was going full throttle, and she couldn't seem to stop it. Everything was out of control—and she liked it.

"Kate, can I see you in my office?"

She picked up her notepad and stepped into Lance's office. It was after hours and much of the staff had gone home.

"Yes, Lance?" she asked. She stopped when she noticed that there was a picnic basket on his desk and a bottle of wine opened and chilling in a wine bucket.

"Join me for dinner?" he asked.

"I guess the boss won't notice if I'm away from desk for a few minutes."

"I already cleared this with the boss."

She closed the door behind her. She didn't want any of their co-workers to see this. Her relationship with Lance was too personal to let the world know about it.

"Then I'd love to join you," she said. "How did you plan all this without me?"

Lance poured her a glass of white wine and handed it to her. "I am capable of doing things on my own."

"I know that. It's just…"

"What?"

"It must have taken some effort for you to surprise me like this…and I didn't think you would do that."

"Why not? I like surprising you," he said.

She wasn't used to this, to this being in a relationship, and she hardly knew what to expect. She'd gone from invisible to this…and it was overwhelming.

"Thank you."

"You're welcome," he said. "I want this to be a special night for you."

Lance was everything she wanted in a man, she thought. She couldn't deny that, no matter how cautious she was trying to be.

Spontaneously, she went up on tiptoe and kissed him. She'd been wanting to all day long.

He caught her close and kissed her back. "Working together is a kind of torture."

"How?" she asked. One hand was roaming up and down her back, the other at the hem of her skirt.

"Seeing you all day, wanting to lift this little skirt of yours and bend you over my desk…" He trailed off as he dropped kisses all along her neck and throat.

"What else do you want to do?" she asked, turned on by the image he'd put in her mind.

"Lots of things, Katie-girl. But I really want to know what you want to do. What is your fantasy?"

"In the office?" she asked.

"We can start there," he said.

"Take your shirt off," she said. Since they'd started sleeping together, she fantasized many times about coming into his office and seeing him sitting there with his shirt off.

"Take my shirt off?"

She nodded.

He reached between them, the backs of his fingers brushing her breasts as he unbuttoned his shirt. She shook from the brief contact and bit her lip to keep from asking for more.

"Now you take yours off," he said.

"Um…I thought I was in charge."

"You are, but I need some incentive to keep on going."

"And if I take my blouse off…"

"I'll be like putty in your hands."

She reached between the two of them and took the hem of her sleeveless sweater in her hands and drew it up over her body. She was wearing a very sexy bra that she'd bought at Becca's store. The cups were all lace and it fastened in the front.

"Very nice," Lance said, running his finger down the center of her body, over her sternum and between her ribs, lingering on her belly button and then stopping at the waistband of her skirt.

He took the front clasp of her bra between his fingers and snapped it open. She stood there on the precipice of something that she couldn't explain. He rubbed his finger over the spot where the clasp had been. The cups were still covering her breasts but she felt…wanton and wicked.

He slowly traced the same path upward again. This time, his fingers feathered under her lacy bra, barely touching her nipples. Both beaded, and a shaft of desire pierced Kate, shaking her.

She needed more. She wanted more. Her heart

beat so swiftly and loudly she was sure he could hear it. She scraped her fingernails lightly down his chest, tangling them in the hair that was there. The dark stuff was tingling against her fingers. He moaned, the sound rumbling up from his chest. He leaned back against his desk, bracing himself on his elbows.

"I'm all yours, Kate," he said.

His muscles jumped under the touch of her fingers as she traced the line down the center of his body. She circled his nipple but didn't touch it, following the fine dusting of hair that narrowed and disappeared into the waistband of his pants.

He pushed the cups of her bra off her breasts. It hung open around them. He pulled her closer until the tips of her breasts brushed his chest.

"Kate." He said her name and she quivered. This was what she'd always wanted from Lance. And now it was hers. He was hers.

His erection nudged her center and she clenched her vagina, wishing he was inside her. She shifted around, trying to feel the tip of his penis against her mound, but it was impossible with her skirt on. Her skirt was hiked up but it wasn't enough.

He kissed his way down her neck and bit lightly at her nape. She shuddered, clutching at his shoulders, grinding her body harder against him.

He found the zipper on the side of her skirt. It loosened as he pushed his hands under the fabric. His big hands slipped into her panties, cupping her butt and urging her to ride him, guiding her motions against his hard-on. He bent his head and his tongue stroked her nipple, and then he suckled her.

Everything in her body tightened. She grabbed Lance's shoulders, rubbing harder and faster against his erection as her climax washed over her. She collapsed against his chest. He held her close. Having Lance act out her fantasy, having him be the man who fulfilled her sexually was more than she'd expected. She wrapped her arms around him, resting her head on his chest and listening to the beat of his heart.

This was more than just a fantasy. This was love—real love—and she didn't know what she'd do if this didn't last.

Lance had never seen anything more beautiful than the passion in Kate. She was more than he'd ever imagined she could be. Her makeover had shown him the woman she was, but the last week he'd helped her realize the woman she could be.

She was exquisitely built. He knew she had body issues, but he loved the imperfection of her. It was what made her a real woman and not some airbrushed ideal that he'd never be able to touch. She was so soft and feminine that she brought out all of his protective instincts, making him want to shield her from the world.

He pushed the straps of her open bra down her arms. Her breasts were full and her skin flushed from her orgasm. Slowly, he caressed her torso, almost afraid to believe that Kate was his.

Her nipples were tight little buds beckoning his mouth. He loved her breasts and couldn't get enough of them.

"I'm sorry," she said, her voice pitched low and a slight blush covering her cheeks and neck.

"For what?"

"Coming without you," she said.

There was something very fragile about Kate and no matter how much headway he made with helping her to realize how much he wanted her, she still was unsure of herself. He pulled her more fully into his arms, cradling her to his chest. She closed her eyes and buried her face in his neck. Each exhalation went through him. He wanted her.

He was so hard and hot for her that he might come in his pants. But he was going to wait for her signal. That was the point of this entire dinner that he'd planned. He wanted some time alone, away from his place, where he could let her have the lead in their relationship.

He felt the minute touches of her tongue against his neck, and his cock hardened. Her hand slid down his chest, opening his belt, unfastening the button at his waistband and then lowering his zipper.

Her hand slid inside his boxers, up and down his length. He tightened his hands on her back. He glanced down his body and saw her small hand burrowed into his pants, saw her working him with such tender care he had to grit his teeth not to end it all right then. But he wanted to be inside her the next time one of them climaxed.

Glancing down, he saw her smiling up at him. He stepped away and laid down the cashmere blanket he'd brought in earlier, urging her over to it. She took a step and her loosened skirt fell off, pooling at her feet. She was left in just her skimpy lace panties and a pair of heels.

"Woman, I wish you could see yourself right now. You'd never doubt your sex appeal again."

She smiled up at him. "It's you," she said.

He leaned down, capturing her mouth with his as he shoved his pants further down his legs and then brought them both down on the blanket, settling down on top of her. She opened her legs and he positioned himself between her thighs.

The humid warmth of her center scorched his already aroused flesh. He thrust against her without thought. Damn, she felt good.

He wanted to enter her totally naked. But they'd had a birth control discussion and she didn't take the pill so that meant he had to keep wearing condoms.

"Can you reach my pants, honey?"

She stretched her arm to grab them. She fished the condom out of his pocket and handed it to him.

He pushed away from her for a minute, rising up on his knees. He glanced over at her and saw she was watching him. Her eyes were on his erection and that made him swell even more. He put the condom on one-handed and turned back to her.

"Hurry, Lance. I need you."

It was the first time she'd asked him to come

to her and he couldn't resist. She opened her arms and her legs, inviting him into her body and he went. He lowered himself over her and rubbed his erection against her mound. He shifted his entire body against hers, caressing her.

She reached between his legs and fondled his sac, cupping him in her hands, and he shuddered. "Don't do that, honey, or I won't last."

She smiled up at him. "Really?"

He wanted to hug her close at the look of wonder on her face. Kate was a joy as a lover because she enjoyed the hell out of him and his body and their lovemaking. "Hell, yes."

He shifted and lifted her thighs, wrapping her legs around his waist. Her hands fluttered between them and their eyes met.

He held her hips steady and entered her slowly. He thrust deeply until he was fully seated. Her eyes widened with each inch he gave her. She clutched at his hips, holding him to her, eyes half-closed and head tipped back.

He leaned down and caught one of her nipples in his teeth, scraping very gently. She started to tighten around him, her hips moving faster, demanding more. But he kept the pace slow, steady, wanting her to come again before he did.

He suckled her nipple and rotated his hips to catch her pleasure point with each thrust, and he felt her hands in his hair as she threw her head back and her climax ripped through her.

He started to thrust faster. He leaned back on his haunches and tipped her hips up to give him deeper access to her body. Her hips were still clenching around his when he felt that tightening at the base of his spine seconds before his body erupted into hers. He pounded into her two, three more times, then collapsed against her. Careful to keep his weight from crushing her, he rolled to his side, taking her with him.

He kept his head at her breast and smoothed his hands down her back. He wanted to just lie here with her in his arms for the rest of the night, but a knock on his office door had them scrambling to their feet.

Kate was horrified that someone was at the door and she and Lance were naked.

"Shh. I've got this. Go stand in the corner and get dressed."

"I can't believe I did this and now we got caught! My mom always said that if I behaved poorly, God would catch me out."

Lance wanted to laugh but knew better. It was just that his mom had said the same thing once. It seemed something all mothers said. And he'd done enough "naughty" things in the course of his life to know that this wasn't God's hand.

"Lance, you in there?" Stan asked.

"Be right there," he said. He pulled his pants up and fastened them.

He found his shirt and put it on. He wasn't about to embarrass Kate by answering the door half-dressed. She was fumbling with her clothes and he wanted—no needed—to get her back into his arms.

"What do you need, Stan?"

"Sorry, sir, but there is a Mr. Martin from the arson investigation here to see you. He's not on the list for the building so we couldn't let him in, and you weren't answering your phone, but you were still in the building according to your logs—"

"Not a problem, Stan. Tell Mr. Martin to have a seat and I'll be down to get him in a few minutes."

"Yes, sir."

He closed the door on Stan and turned back

to find Kate completely dressed. Her arms were wrapped around her waist and she watched him with those wide eyes of hers. Only right now they seemed wounded and scared.

"Can we postpone our dinner?"

"Yes," she said. "I need to clean up in the washroom and then—"

He stopped her with a finger over her lips. "Why don't you go home, honey? I'll stop by when this is over."

She shook her head. "I think I need to be alone tonight."

"Why?"

"Because I need to reflect on this. That sounds silly, doesn't it?"

"Not really."

"Good. Because I want to make sense of this. Changing my image is one thing, but changing my core values…that's something different."

"Making love with the man you are dating isn't a change in your values."

"Yes, it is, Lance. I wouldn't be in this situation with any other man."

"Why not?"

"Because you're the one I love," she said, and turned on her heel to walk away.

"Wait a minute, Kate."

She stopped, but didn't turn back. He wanted to say the hell with Martin and just keep her here until they finished this discussion.

But the refinery was his top priority right now. He was torn. For the first time since he'd taken over Brody Oil and Gas, a woman was coming between him and his responsibilities.

"Not now, Lance."

"You love me?"

"Yes," she said. "And I have to decide if I still want to have an affair with my boss. Because when Stan knocked on that door, all the love I felt for you was embarrassing and I don't want that."

"You shouldn't be embarrassed. Stan doesn't know you were in here or what we were doing," Lance said.

"But I do. And I'm the one who will bare the shame of it. I don't want to feel ashamed of anything between us. I hadn't before but then all of a sudden…"

Lance understood. He realized that he needed to make this relationship between them more permanent. But he couldn't until he broke things off with Lexi. He'd hoped to do that face to face, but a phone call might have to do it.

He pulled her back into his arms and refused to let her go. "Kate, I'm not hiding you or ashamed of you."

"I know that, Lance. But I have been hiding. I know half the office has always guessed that I was in love with you and now…well, now it seems like you just noticed me since I'm…sexy."

He was proud of her for thinking she was sexy. It was a complete turn around for her.

"Well, you are sexy. But that's not what this is about. Listen, I have to wrap things up with Lexi. Then you and I can—"

"What do you mean you have to wrap things up with her?" Kate asked.

"I haven't had a chance to talk to her yet. It's not a big deal."

"Are you still engaged?" Kate asked.

"Not to my way of thinking," Lance said.

Kate pulled away and put her hands on her hips. "To anyone's way of thinking…are you engaged?"

Lance looked down at her. This night was certainly not going his way. But he hadn't lied to Kate from the beginning and he wasn't about to start now.

"Yes, I am still engaged."

Her lip quivered and her face lost all color. "I can't believe this. I'm an idiot."

She turned on her heel and he stopped her once again. "You aren't. I meant everything I said to you."

"Really? Because the only way for that to be true is for me to be your mistress. Is that what you had in mind for us?"

"No," he said.

Lance's phone started ringing and he knew he had to answer it. Damn it. "This is not over, Kate."

"Yes, Lance, it is."

Nine

Kate looked down at the speedometer and realized she was driving way too fast. Anger had gotten the better of her, and she could still feel the flush of shame on her cheeks. She forced herself to slow down.

A part of her sort of understood where Lance was coming from. She got that he might be waiting to talk to Lexi in person to break their engagement. And if he felt for her even a tenth of what she did for him, then the emotions and the attraction would have been hard to resist, engaged or not.

But the main thing that was bothering her was her own reactions. She'd forgotten who she was. Her new clothes and hair and make-up had made her feel like she was a different person.

And it was only as she'd been standing in the corner of Lance's office, trying to quickly get back into her clothes, that she'd realized she was making a mistake.

Love shouldn't feel like this, she thought as she turned into the garage of her town house. She parked her car and went inside.

Love should be something to be celebrated and shared. And for so long she was used to her love for Lance being her dirty little secret. It hadn't occurred to her that she'd allowed that to become the rule for their relationship. She'd been used to hiding it and had allowed herself to be hidden.

The last week had been wonderful but she realized tonight that she wanted more.

She looked at the bracelet he'd given her. She knew that he didn't think less of her than he did before. But she had no idea what he really wanted from her. Did he just want to continue their affair until it ran its course?

And was she willing to keep working for him—and sleeping with him?

That was the problem with being a modern woman, she thought. The lines in these situations were blurred. And she didn't know which way to turn.

She turned the air-conditioner down and walked through the house to the shower. She washed, wishing she could wipe away the memories of Lance's body inside of hers, of that closeness that they'd had together for too short a time.

She put on a sundress and walked through her home. She'd decorated it with antiques that she and her mom had found in Canton up near Dallas, and with photos of her family. But there was nothing that was really hers in it, much like the new clothing had been window dressing for a person she wanted to be. This house was what she'd always imagined a city girl would have.

But she'd never made that city girl's life her own. Now she wanted to. No, she needed to if she had even the slightest hope of surviving this love she had for Lance.

She didn't know the depth of her love for him before this month. Now she loved the way he smiled at her when no one else could see them. She loved the way he went out of his way to surprise her and she loved the way he made her feel like she was it—the only woman in the world that he wanted to see and spend time with.

And that kind of love…well, it wasn't going to go away. So she had to figure this out. Could she continue her affair with him while he was still engaged?

There was a knock on her door an hour later and she knew who it was without even looking through the peephole.

She unlocked the door and opened it, but stood in the doorway. "Lance."

"Can I come in?"

She tipped her head to the side, considering it. He'd been to her place once before but never as her lover. All of their trysts—what an old-fashioned word, she thought—had taken place at Lance's.

She decided to let him in. Obviously they needed to talk. "Sure. Is everything okay with the investigation?"

"Yes. Mr. Martin was getting some restless employees at the fire scene one he needed me to keep them clear."

She led the way into her living room and heard him close the front door behind him. She sat down in the Kennedy rocker that had been her grandmother's and took a sip of lemonade.

"Can I get you a drink?"

"A beer would be great," Lance said. She noticed he had the picnic basket in his hands. "Have you eaten?"

"No, I haven't," she said.

"I'll set this up while you go get my beer. I am starved. It has been a really long day."

"Yes, it has," Kate said. Sleeping with the boss took a lot out of her. She didn't like the way that sounded—even to herself. She found a Coors Light in the fridge and brought it out to Lance. He smiled at her as he took it.

He took a long draw from the bottle, then set it on the coaster on the coffee table.

The food he'd put out was a cold pasta and chicken salad. It was exactly the kind of dinner she liked on a hot July night and she didn't kid herself that Lance hadn't planned it that way.

He was a man who noticed things.

"Thanks for dinner," she said, as she sat down beside him on the couch and picked up her fork.

Kate steered the conversation to work and to

Mitch, who was due back from DC by the end
of the week. She did her level best to make sure
that they didn't have a chance to talk about her
confession of love.

But then they finished their meal and Lance
leaned back against the couch, stretching his long
arms along the back of it. "So you love me?"

Lance had thought of nothing else during his
drive over to her place. No woman had ever told
him she loved him. And that included his fiancée
and his mother. He wasn't a man who went out
searching for the softer things in life. He took
what he wanted and let the devil take the rest.

But he wanted Kate's love.

Now that she'd said she loved him, he wanted
to hear her say it again. And he wanted to take
her and have her say it while he was buried hilt
deep in her sexy little body.

"I…yes, I do love you, but that doesn't mean
that I'm going to just let you walk all over me."

"I didn't think for a moment that it did. Actually I have no idea what it means."

"What are you saying?"

"Just that love isn't something I've had a lot
of experience with."

"Well, you're the only guy I've ever loved so I guess neither of us knows much about this," she said.

But Kate knew love better than Lance did. He knew she'd come from the kind of family that people liked to complain about but was filled with love.

"And I'm not sure that's a good thing," Kate said.

"Why not?"

"Because love shouldn't be one-sided. It's not healthy."

"Listen, Kate, I'm not about to promise you something I can't deliver." Losing Kate wasn't something he was prepared to do. Having had her, he didn't know if he'd ever be ready to let her walk out the door.

"I appreciate that, Lance. But I have to do what's healthy for me, too. I just can't keep loving a man who never puts me first."

"That's not fair. I've put you first."

"Yes, but in the privacy of your office or your home," Kate said quietly.

She was tired of being hidden from the world, which suited him fine—he got that. But he didn't want Kate to think she could manipulate him into doing whatever she wanted. It was important to him that she let him take the lead in their relationship.

"What can I say?"

She bit her lip and then leaned forward so that her face was turned away from him and her arms rested on her knees.

"If I have to tell you, then I guess that means there isn't anything to say."

Lance wasn't sure what she wanted. Hell, that was a lie, he knew exactly what she wanted. "I'm not going to say I love you, Kate. I just told you I have no experience with that emotion."

"I don't understand how you can say that. You have dated a lot of women."

"None of them have loved me."

"Well, your mother did and your father, too, right? And Mitch loves you."

Lance shrugged. The devotion his brother and he had didn't fit into the mold of what he'd call love. It was just a bond that had been forged in the fire of their upbringing. And there was little in the world that would change that. "I don't know. What's between Mitch and me isn't like you saying you love me."

"Why not?" she asked.

"Because I want you to love me. That feels right to me, Kate. A part of me thinks you belong to me. Right or wrong, that's the way I feel."

"Belong to you?" she asked.

He nodded. What would he do if she said to get out? Not just out of her house but out of her life? He'd just told her that she was his. And she was. That was as much as he could feel for a woman.

"I like the thought of being yours, Lance. But I'm confused."

"I can appreciate that. What would it take to clear things up for you?"

"You are still engaged to Lexi," Kate said.

"I'm ending that, Kate. I can't marry another woman when I'm involved with you."

Lance realized in that moment that he'd do whatever she asked if it was in his power. He needed everything in his relationship with Kate to be resolved. It was past time for him to figure out what he wanted as a man.

And everything kept pointing to Kate.

"I guess I need some time to think about that," she said. "I feel like I've been loving you forever and maybe it's time to figure out what that really means to me—and to you."

Lance didn't like the sound of that. But he wasn't about to beg for her affection. He'd heard too many fights between his parents that had gone the same way.

"I'm not going to play games with you, Kate. If you want to be with me—if you love me—then I think you can put a little effort into being with me."

Kate crossed her arms over her chest. She looked at him and he knew he'd said the wrong thing. "I've been loving you for a long time, Lance Brody, and you never even knew I was alive. So you do what you have to. I'm not playing games with you. I'm just standing up for myself. And I don't like you trying to push me around."

"I'm not pushing you around," Lance said.

He should have guessed that her love wasn't real. It was probably tied to the sexuality of their relationship and the fact that he was the first man to make her feel like a woman.

Kate shook her head. "I didn't say you were doing anything wrong. I just need to think. And you need to end things with Lexi. I'm not going to stop loving you overnight, Lance."

"Well, I'm not too sure about that. It seems

like you have a checklist of things I need to do to win your love and once we check them all off you'll be mine." Lance stood up and walked to the front door. "I guess you haven't changed as much as you'd like to think you have because you are still standing on the sidelines of life, waiting for it to happen to you."

Kate watched Lance walk away and fought not to call him back. But he'd lied to her. He was still engaged to another woman and worst of all, he didn't love her.

She closed the door and went back inside. She walked through the quietness of the living room, seeing the remains of their dinner.

She didn't understand how a man could be so perfect that she'd fall in love with him, and yet so disappointing.

She didn't know if it was just a sop for her heart or not, but she couldn't force herself to believe that Lance didn't care for her at least a little bit. Even if he didn't call it love.

Her house phone rang and she checked the caller ID.

"Hello, Lance."

"Listen, Kate. I'm not sure what I said back

there that made things get out of control the way they did. But I don't want to end this relationship."

Kate didn't, either. But as she looked around her lonely little town house she knew they couldn't continue the way they had been. There was a reason why Lance's engagement had spurred her into action. A reason why she'd been motivated to change things that she'd been content to leave before. And that reason was that she'd finally figured out that no man—especially not Lance—was going to fall in love with her if she just kept being there.

"I can't do this right now. I really need to think."

"Can't do what?"

"Talk to you. Because I'll agree to whatever you say and that's not healthy. Not for either one of us. You said you didn't know what love was, hadn't experienced it like this, and I know what you meant."

"What did I mean?"

He'd meant that he'd never had anyone like her in his life, someone who'd been so in love with him that they'd take whatever scraps of affection he threw their way. But she was done with that. She had more pride than that…she deserved better.

"You meant that it was okay for me to keep loving you," she said.

"More than okay," Lance said.

"Why? Do you love me?" Kate asked.

He hesitated and she had her answer.

"Damn it, Kate. I don't know what to say. I want you like I've never wanted any other woman," Lance said.

That didn't matter. Her physical appearance could change. Would that mean he wouldn't want her anymore?

"That's not enough."

"It's a start," Lance said.

"Yes, I guess it is. But I want the man I love to love me back. I want you to need to be with me the way I need to be with you."

"Katie-girl, you are making this more difficult than it has to be. Let me come back to your place and I'll prove to you that I need you just as much as you need me."

Kate was tempted to say yes. She almost did, but then she thought about the fact that sex wasn't love. It didn't mean that it couldn't be but with Lance, right now sex was just sex, no matter how good it was.

"I don't mean making love, Lance."

"Making love—you just said it yourself. It's an expression of our emotions."

"Ours? Do you love me?"

"Hell, girl, I just said I don't know."

"I know. I was pushing and I'm sorry. But I just don't know what else to do. You broke my heart when you got engaged. And tonight I found out you are still engaged."

She was rambling, so she just stopped talking. But she knew that some element of truth had been revealed there. She couldn't just keep loving him. Not now that she'd realized that he didn't really love her. And not now that she knew he was still engaged to Lexi.

"I'm not going to marry Lexi Cavanaugh, Kate. I can't marry another woman if I'm involved with you."

"Good. That makes me feel better. But until things are resolved between the two of you, I have to keep my distance."

"Why?"

Kate thought about it. She'd left the office feeling ashamed and didn't like that. And she knew it stemmed from the fact that she wasn't sure that Lance was her man.

She needed that certainty. If she had that then

everything they did together would be motivated by love. And that would be enough for her.

"I just have to. I'm sorry."

Silence buzzed over the open line and she wondered what Lance was thinking. No matter how well she'd come to know him over the last week, he was still an enigma to her.

And she realized that he probably always would be. That was part of what had made her fall in love with him to begin with. There were secrets and pain in Lance Brody's eyes and those very things had drawn her to him.

No matter what she did she had a feeling she was always going to love him.

"Goodbye, Lance."

He cursed under his breath. "Are you quitting Brody Oil and Gas, as well as quitting me?"

"Yes. I am. I won't be coming back to the office at all. In fact, I need to get away from Houston."

"You do that," he said. "Run away if you think that will help. But to be honest, I don't believe it will."

"How would you know?"

Lance didn't strike her as a man who'd run away from anything.

"My mother did it and I don't think she was any happier after she left us."

Lance hung up before she could say anything else. Kate was faced with the fact that she'd hurt Lance more deeply than she'd imagined she could. But she couldn't keep putting him first. She needed to take care of her heart, which felt as if it had been broken in two.

Ten

Figuring that this evening wasn't going to get any better, Lance put a call in to Lexi. He got her voice mail and even he knew better than to break an engagement via a message, so he simply asked her to call him back.

He didn't want to go home or to the office. Those two places were haunted by Kate even in his mind. Instead he drove to the Texas Cattleman's Club. Drinking with his buddies was exactly what he needed.

He tossed his keys to the valet and went

straight inside to the game room. He needed a drink and a game to set his mind straight.

His cell phone rang as he went to the self-service wet bar and poured himself a whiskey.

The area code was Virginia. That could only mean Lexi.

"Brody here," he said, answering the phone.

"It's Lexi. I got your message. What did you need to talk to me about?"

Lance took a swallow of his drink and sank down onto one of the large leather chairs.

"I wanted to have a word with you about our engagement," he said.

"Good. Father was asking me about it earlier today and I told him we hadn't talked about the arrangements. I know we didn't talk about dates but I was thinking the sooner the better."

Lance felt like an ass. There was no other way to put it. But he couldn't make the same mistake his father had. That marriage to his mother had ruined the old man. And may have been the trigger to all that anger in him.

"Lexi…I don't know how to say this."

"Say what?" she asked. "I was at Papyrus earlier today and found some beautiful invitations.

I am having them send you a sample so you can let me know if you approve or not."

This was getting worse by the second. He took a deep breath.

"Lexi, I can't marry you."

"What?"

"I'm sorry. But I am involved with another woman and I…" Lance choked on the words he had to say. *He loved Kate.* Hell. He loved her. Suddenly all of his doubts were gone and he knew why he couldn't let Kate go.

Love.

The one emotion he'd never let himself experience until Kate. That was why nothing had seemed right earlier when he was walking away. But Kate was the first person who should hear those words.

"I just can't marry you feeling the way I do about someone else."

"Who is it?"

"Kate Thornton."

"Your secretary. Lance, please, men of your station don't marry secretaries."

"I don't care. Kate's the woman I can't get out of my mind and I would make all of us miserable if I went through with a marriage to you."

Lexi was silent, and Lance knew that this wasn't the best way to deliver this kind of news. He should call Mitch and ask him to go to her and make this right.

"I'm very sorry."

"I am, too. My father really wanted this marriage."

"I know. And if it means he can't back the bill we asked him to then we will have to find another way to expand our operation. I just know that I don't want to consign either of us to a miserable life."

He took another swallow of his drink and then realized the truth he'd just spoken. Happiness was very important to him. He'd been searching for the happiness that had eluded him his entire life, and he wasn't going to find it unless Kate was by his side.

"I guess there's nothing more to say to you," Lexi said.

"I am sorry. But I think that you'll thank me for this one day."

"Please don't say that. This isn't something that I'm going to recover from easily."

"I didn't realize that you cared for me," Lance said.

"Well, I wouldn't have agreed to marry you if I didn't."

"Lexi—"

"I'm being cruel. You are a stranger to me as I am to you. I don't blame you for breaking this off."

She hung up and he sat there, feeling as if his life was like this empty room. And it had been for a while now. But he knew how to fill it.

The answer was Kate. But before he could go to her he had to take care of Lexi, had to make sure that Mitch ran interference with the senator.

He dialed his brother's cell phone. Mitch had just gotten back from DC. And he knew his brother wasn't going to be pleased.

"Its Mitch."

"I broke off my engagement with Lexi Cavanaugh," Lance said.

"What?! Why?"

"I couldn't marry her feeling the way I do about Kate."

"Kate? Since when do you care about her?" Mitch asked. "Does Lexi know this?"

"I just called her and she sounded upset. Listen, I know it may have complicated things with the senator but I think I love Kate and I can't let her slip through my fingers."

"This does more than complicate things, Lance. Damn it. I wish you'd spoken to me before you called Lexi."

"I'm sorry."

"You should be. I have no idea how I'm going to fix this. We need the senator on our side," Mitch said.

"If anyone can figure out how to make this work, it's you."

"I will figure it out. So you love Kate?" Mitch asked.

"Yes, I do. Damn it. I wanted her to be the first one I told."

"Well, what are you waiting for? Go tell her."

Lance was nervous as he drove to Kate's town house. He had no idea what to say. For once he had no idea how to handle a situation. This wasn't at all what he was used to. But then neither was Kate. And he was damned sure whatever happened he was going to make her listen to him.

When he got to her town house it was empty and her car was long gone. Where was she?

Lance searched for Kate for as long as he could but then realized he needed a professional.

He called Darius the next morning around ten. He stood in his office, unable to sit at his desk without seeing Kate as she'd been last night when she'd taken control of their lovemaking. He'd never realized that a woman could complete him on so many levels.

"It's Lance."

"Hey. I don't have any news on your fire," Darius said. Lance heard the sounds of a radio in the background.

"I'm not calling about that. I need a favor."

"Another one? They are stacking up. You are going to owe me."

"Yes, I am. But this is important."

"What do you need?"

Lance took a deep breath. "Kate Thornton is missing and I need you to find her."

"Okay, did you call the cops?" Darius asked.

"No. I don't think there has been foul play. I just need to find her and she's not taking my calls."

Darius started laughing. "You've got woman troubles."

"Yes, Darius, I do. And this woman—I need to find her. She's not like anyone else."

"Seriously?"

"Yes."

"Okay, I will help you. Give me her cell number."

Lance rattled off the number.

"Did you try her friends and family?"

"I called Becca Huntington, her best friend, but only got voice mail. And her parents haven't heard from her."

Lance looked out of the skyscraper window, wondering where the hell she was. He needed her and she wasn't here. He was going to tell her about this moment when he had her back in his arms.

Love should mean that they could count on each other. He knew she was hurting and that was why she'd left, but he needed her back.

"Give me a chance to work on this and I'll get back to you."

"Thanks, Darius."

"You're welcome, man."

Darius hung up and Lance paced around his office. He should be working. Work had always been his refuge when life got complicated but he just couldn't make himself do it this time. The only thing he could think about was Kate.

He saw her as she'd been when he'd first come back from DC, with her horn-rimmed glasses and baggy clothes. He pictured her in that short skirt and sleeveless sweater of yesterday and he realized that he'd cared about Kate for a long time. He just hadn't been paying attention.

His phone rang in the midafternoon. It was Darius.

"I've found her."

"Great. Tell me where she is."

"I think you need a plan. What are you going to do when you see her?" Darius asked.

"Tell her that she can't leave again and that she's mine."

"That's a horrible plan. Women need finesse," Darius said. "Stay in your office. I'm on my way over there."

Darius hung up before Lance could argue. Mitch walked into his office ten minutes later.

"What are you doing?" Mitch asked.

Lance had been pacing since Darius's call. "Waiting for Darius. He found Kate but he thinks… He's right I need a plan."

"What are you going to do?" Mitch asked.

Lance knew there was only one thing he could do at this point. He loved Kate and he wanted her to be his wife. "I'm going to tell her we are getting married."

Mitch nodded. "It makes sense. But I think you need to do it right this time. Kate's loved you forever."

"How do you know that?" Lance asked.

"Everyone knows that. I think you're the reason she stayed with us in the lean years. You've always been the man for her."

"I have?" Lance felt like he should have noticed this. No wonder Kate had reacted the way she had to his engagement to another woman. "I want to make this engagement the stuff of her dreams."

"Do you know what her dreams are?" Mitch asked.

He didn't. But he did know that Kate appreciated romantic gestures. The idea came to him then. He'd ask her to marry him in the formal dining room of the Texas Cattleman's Club. He would fill the space with candles and flowers and make it as romantic as he could.

He wanted Kate to know from the moment she stepped inside that he loved her. He wanted her to feel like the years she'd spent waiting for him to find her were worth it.

Because they were to him.

"Will you do me a favor?" he asked Mitch.

"Another favor," Darius said from the door. "You better hope we don't all call them in on the same day."

"Good, you're here. Mitch?"

"Sure, I'll help you out," Mitch said.

"Great. This is what I need you to do."

He told his brother and his best friend his plan, knowing that this was the way a man should get engaged. He should have his friends and family by his side, not be alone in a hotel room in a strange city.

Mitch agreed to go get Kate and bring her to the Cattleman's Club. Darius agreed to go get the ring that Lance had ordered from a downtown jeweler. And Lance went to the club to make sure every detail was perfect when Kate arrived.

Kate worked out in the Ritz's exercise room and then grabbed a bottle of water before heading for the elevator. She'd needed to get away, but going home to her parents hadn't seemed right. She really didn't want to travel anywhere so she'd packed a bag and come here.

She could be pampered, and order room service and forget about Lance Brody—except it wasn't working. Not at all. She'd woken from her sleep missing his arms around her.

She couldn't sleep without his chest under her cheek and the soothing beating of his heart in her ear. She wondered if she'd made the biggest mistake of her life in letting him go.

But at the same time, she knew there was no future for them unless she'd stood her ground.

And so here she was, on her ground and alone.

Being by herself wasn't a big deal, but being lonely was. She felt bereft, like she didn't know who she was or what she wanted.

Kate waited for the elevator feeling more out of place than she ever had before. And it wasn't the opulent surroundings that made her feel that way. It was her own emotions.

Lance had been her constant for so long, and a big part of her had believed that he always would be. She didn't know who she was if she didn't love Lance. And that was a big part of her problem. Getting over him was going to take longer than a week and she wondered if, having loved him and been his lover, she ever could.

The elevator arrived and she got in, pushing the number for her floor. When she arrived there, she got off and saw a man standing in the hallway near her room.

From the back he was almost as tall as Lance and for a minute her heart stopped beating, thinking it might be him. But then she realized how silly that was. Lance didn't know where she was.

As she got closer, she recognized the man as Mitch. He was on the phone but looked up as she approached.

He disconnected his call and put his phone in his pocket.

"I bet you are wondering why I am here."

"Yes, I am."

"Can we talk in your room?"

She nodded and moved past him to her door. She put her keycard in and then led the way into the bedroom. Mitch sat down in one of the guest chairs and she sat on the bed.

"Lance asked me to come."

"Why?"

"He needs to see you."

"And he couldn't come himself," Kate said. "You are your brother's emissary a lot." But she was elated. Lance had taken the only step he could to make their relationship work.

"I know, and I think its time I stopped speaking for him," Mitch said. "I've got a lot of work to do back in DC to fix the mess his broken engagement caused."

Kate nibbled her lower lip. "I'm sorry, Mitch."

He shook his head. "Don't be. Lance was always the man for you."

She shrugged. "I don't know about that any longer. I'm not sure where we stand."

"That's why he sent me here. He needs to talk to you face to face and since you weren't answering his calls, he figured an invitation from me would serve him better than another voice mail."

"I didn't mean to be childish," Kate said. "I just needed time to think. I don't know if you can understand this, Mitch, but when you love someone the way I do Lance, it makes you weak."

"Give Lance a chance to make it up to you," Mitch said. "Whatever he did to cause a rift between you, I know he's committed to making it right."

"I'm not sure he can. I want things from him… I guess you don't need to know this."

"I don't suppose I do," Mitch said. "But if you need to talk then don't stop."

She shook her head. She didn't need to talk to anyone except for Lance. "Where is he?"

"At the Texas Cattleman's Club in Somerset. You are invited to join him for dinner in the main dining room."

"Okay, I don't know where the club is."

Mitch laughed. "I'm going to escort you there."

"That's okay, Mitch. I can find my own way. Just leave the address for me."

"Are you sure?"

She nodded. "What time do I need to be there?"

"At six."

Mitch left and Kate took a shower. She got dressed, taking her time with her hair and make-up. She hadn't brought a formal dress with her but a quick call to the boutique downstairs fixed that. Soon she was dressed in a stunningly gorgeous cocktail dress and sexy heels.

And as she caught a glimpse of herself in the mirror, she realized that for the first time the outer woman matched the inner one. Regardless of what Lance said to her tonight, she was finally at peace with who she was.

Eleven

Kate gave her keys to the valet at the club and followed his directions to take the stairs to the entryway. She held her evening bag in one hand and fiddled nervously with the bracelet on her wrist.

She walked slowly up the steps in the heat of the Texas summer evening, feeling the weight of her hair against her bare back as she moved. A doorman opened the door for her as she approached and she smiled her thanks.

"Good evening, ma'am. May I help you?"

"I'm here for dinner with Lance Brody."

The man smiled at her. "Of course, right this way."

He led her to the left of the anteroom and then stopped at the bottom of the stairs. The club was a converted mansion and though Kate had heard about it before, this was the first time she'd been inside.

She noticed red rose petals on the stairs in a path.

"Follow the petals, ma'am."

She did, holding on to the banister for support as she climbed the stairs. She was speechless at the amount of planning Lance had done for this night. And she had a feeling that no matter what he said, she wasn't going to be able to walk away from him.

She got to the top of the stairs and saw Darius waiting for her.

"Hello, Kate. You look very nice tonight."

"Hi, Darius. What are you doing here?"

"Another favor for Lance. That boy is going to owe me big-time."

Darius offered her his arm and escorted her to

the main dining room. The room was lit only by candles, and fresh flowers had been placed on every table.

Darius led her to the table in the center of the room that had been set for dinner. He seated her.

"Lance will be here in a few moments. He wanted you to have this."

Darius handed her a white envelope. Her name was scrawled across the outside in Lance's spidery writing.

Darius walked away as she slid her finger under the flap of the envelope to open it. She pulled out a card which had a picture of the two of them from the Fourth.

Inside was a simple message.

I'm sorry. Your love is a precious gift and I'm blessed to have it.

She put the card down and turned to see Lance approaching. He wore a suit and looked so good in it. He was so handsome and sexy that she felt tears burn the back of her eyes because she knew that Lance Brody was her man, that he belonged to her.

"Hello, Kate."

"Thank you for the card," she said.

"You're welcome. I'm sorry things got out of hand the way they did."

She shook her head. "It's okay. I think I expected you to catch up to all the feelings I'd had for you for so long. But that was expecting too much."

Lance reached down and pulled her to her feet. He kissed her softly on her lips. "No, it wasn't."

He hugged her close in his arms and whispered in her ear. "I love you, Kate Thornton. I don't know how I didn't recognize it before this. But I can't live without you by my side."

She pulled back to look into his eyes. She needed to make sure that he believed what he was telling her, and she saw his love reflected there. She hugged him even closer and closed her eyes, afraid that she was dreaming this entire thing.

But Lance's arms around her were solid and real, and his scent filled every breath she took.

"Have a seat, Kate," he said.

She sat down and Lance got on his knee next to her. He took her hands in his and lifted them to his mouth to kiss them.

"Will you marry me, Kate?"

She stared down at him for a nanosecond before she said, "Yes!"

She stood up and Lance did, too. Kate threw herself in his arms and hugged him close to her, knowing that she'd found the man of her dreams.

Mitch and Darius congratulated them both, and Lance decided that they shouldn't wait to get married. He wanted to go by private jet to Vegas that very night.

"I can't get married without my best friend," Kate said.

"That's why I called her. Becca?"

Becca stepped into the room, smiling at her. "I've even invited your parents."

Since Lance had thought of everything, there was nothing else to do but say yes.

Lance stood in the wedding chapel at the Bellagio Hotel, waiting for his bride. His brother was standing next to him, and his best friend was seated next to Kate's parents.

He was filled with such joy and love for Kate that he knew this was the right thing to do. This was the way a man should feel when he thinks of his fiancée. And he knew that he'd asked the right woman to marry him this time.

The minister that they'd hired for the event smiled at him, and Lance felt a sense of rightness in his world that had long been missing. He and Mitch had been lucky in business and had the devil's own luck when it came to finding new wells, but this was the first time he'd felt lucky in love.

The music started, and Darius and Kate's parents stood up. Becca Huntington walked down the aisle first but then Kate stepped out and he stopped breathing. She was exquisite, this woman who was going to be his wife.

She walked slowly toward him and Lance couldn't see anyone but her. The minister went through the ceremony but Lance was just waiting for the end, waiting to kiss her and claim her as his for now and forever.

They exchanged I do's.

"I now pronounce you man and wife," the minister said. "You may kiss your bride."

Lance looked down into Kate's face and saw the love shining there in her eyes. He took her mouth with his and kissed her, showing her how happy she'd made him and what this evening meant to him.

Darius and Mitch clapped as they made their union official.

"I love you, Mrs. Lance Brody," Lance said.

Kate beamed at him. "Well, it's about time," she said, pulling him into another kiss.

* * * * *

Don't miss THE WEALTHY RANCHER,
The next installment of
THE TEXAS GENTLEMAN'S CLUB!
Available next month from Silhouette Desire.

*Celebrate 60 years of pure reading pleasure
with Harlequin!*

To commemorate the event, Harlequin Intrigue® is thrilled to invite you to the wedding of The Colby Agency's J. T. Baxley and his bride, Eve Mattson.

That is, of course, if J.T. can find the woman who left him at the altar. Considering he's a private investigator for one of the top agencies in the country—the best of the best—that shouldn't be a problem. The real setback is that his bride isn't who she appears to be…and her mysterious past has put them both in danger.

The dark figures on the dock were still firing. The bullets cutting through the surface of the water without the warning boom of shots told Eve they were using silencers.

That was to her benefit. Silencers decreased the accuracy of every shot and lessened the range.

She grabbed for the rocks. Scrambled through the darkness. Bumped her knee on a boulder. Cursed.

Burrowing into the waist-deep grass, she kept

low and crawled forward. Faster. Pushed harder. Needed as much distance as possible.

Shots pinged on the rocks.

J.T. scrambled alongside her.

He was breathing hard.

They had to stay close to the ground until they reached the next row of warehouses. Even though she was relatively certain they were out of range at this point, she wasn't taking any risks. And she wasn't slowing down.

J.T. had to keep up.

The splat of a bullet hitting the ground next to Eve had her rolling left. Maybe they weren't completely out of range.

She bumped J.T. He grunted.

His injured arm. Dammit. She could apologize later.

Half a dozen more yards.

Almost in the clear.

As she reached the cover of the alley between the first two warehouses she tensed.

Silence.

No pings or splats.

She glanced back at the dock. Deserted.

Time to run.

Her car was parked another block down.

Pushing to her feet, she sprinted forward. The wet bag dragged at her shoulder. She ignored it.

By the time she reached the lot where her car was parked, she had dug the keys from her pocket and hit the fob. Six seconds later she was behind the wheel. She hit the ignition as J.T. collapsed into the passenger seat. Tires squealed as she spun out of the slot.

"What the hell did you do to me?"

From the corner of her eye she watched him shake his head in an attempt to clear it.

He would be pissed when she told him about the tranquilizer.

She'd needed him cooperative until she formulated a plan. A drug-induced state of unconsciousness had been the fastest and most efficient method to ensure his continued solidarity.

"I can't really talk right now." Eve weaved into the right lane as the street widened to four lanes. What she needed was traffic. It was Saturday night—shouldn't be that difficult to find as soon as they were out of the old warehouse district.

A glance in the rearview mirror warned that their unwanted company had caught up.

Sensing her tension, J.T. turned to peer over his left shoulder.

"I hope you have a plan B."

She shot him a look. "There's always plan G." Then she pulled the Glock out of her waistband.

Cutting the steering wheel left, she slid between two vehicles. Another veer to the right and she'd put several cars between hers and the enemy.

She was betting they wouldn't pull out the firepower in the open like this, but a girl could never be too sure when it came to an unknown enemy.

Deep blending was the way to go.

Two traffic lights ahead the marquis of a movie theater provided exactly the opportunity she was looking for.

The digital numbers on the dash indicated it was just past midnight. Perfect timing. The late movie would be purging its audience into the crowd of teenagers who liked hanging out in the parking lot.

She took a hard right onto the property that sported a twelve-screen theater, numerous fast-food hot spots and a chain superstore. Speeding across the lot, she selected a lane of parking slots. Pulling in as close to the theater entrance as possible, she shut off the engine and reached for her door.

"Let's go."

Thankfully he didn't argue.

Rounding the hood of her car, she shoved the Glock into her bag, then wrapped her arm around J.T.'s and merged into the crowd.

With her free hand she finger-combed her long hair. It was soaked, as were her clothes. The kids she bumped into noticed, gave her death-ray glares.

They just didn't know.

As she and J.T. moved in closer to the building, she grabbed a baseball cap from an innocent bystander. The crowd made it easy. The kid who owned the cap had made it even easier by stuffing the cap bill-first into his waistband at the small of his back.

Pushing through the loitering crowd, she made her way to the side of the building next to the main entrance. She pushed J.T. against the wall and dropped her bag to the ground. Peeled off her tee and let it fall.

His gaze instantly zeroed in on her breasts, where the cami she wore had glued to her skin like an extra layer. A zing of desire shot through her veins.

Not the time.

With a flick of her wrist she twisted her hair up and clamped the cap atop the blond mass.

"They're coming," J.T. muttered as he gazed at some point beyond her.

"Yeah, I know." She planted her palms against the wall on either side of him and leaned in. "Keep your eyes open. Let me know when they're inside."

Then she planted her lips on his.

* * * * *

Will J.T. and Eve be caught in the moment?
Or will Eve get the chance to reveal
all of her secrets?
Find out in
THE BRIDE'S SECRETS
by Debra Webb
Available August 2009
from Harlequin Intrigue®.

We'll be spotlighting a different series every month throughout 2009 to celebrate our 60th anniversary.

LOOK FOR
HARLEQUIN INTRIGUE®
IN AUGUST!

To commemorate the event, Harlequin Intrigue® is thrilled to invite you to the wedding of the Colby Agency's J. T. Baxley and his bride, Eve Mattson.

Look for *Colby Agency: Elite Reconnaissance*

THE BRIDE'S SECRETS
BY DEBRA WEBB

Available August 2009

THBPA0108

REQUEST YOUR FREE BOOKS!

2 FREE NOVELS PLUS 2 FREE GIFTS!

Silhouette®

Desire®

Passionate, Powerful, Provocative!

YES! Please send me 2 FREE Silhouette Desire® novels and my 2 FREE gifts (gifts are worth about $10). After receiving them, if I don't wish to receive any more books, I can return the shipping statement marked "cancel". If I don't cancel, I will receive 6 brand-new novels every month and be billed just $4.05 per book in the U.S. or $4.74 per book in Canada. That's a savings of almost 15% off the cover price! It's quite a bargain! Shipping and handling is just 50¢ per book.* I understand that accepting the 2 free books and gifts places me under no obligation to buy anything. I can always return a shipment and cancel at any time. Even if I never buy another book, the two free books and gifts are mine to keep forever.   225 SDN EYMS   326 SDN EYM4

Name	(PLEASE PRINT)	
Address		Apt. #
City	State/Prov.	Zip/Postal Code

Signature (if under 18, a parent or guardian must sign)

Mail to the **Silhouette Reader Service:**
IN U.S.A.: P.O. Box 1867, Buffalo, NY 14240-1867
IN CANADA: P.O. Box 609, Fort Erie, Ontario L2A 5X3

Not valid to current subscribers of Silhouette Desire books.

Want to try two free books from another line?
Call 1-800-873-8635 or visit www.morefreebooks.com.

* Terms and prices subject to change without notice. Prices do not include applicable taxes. Sales tax applicable in N.Y. Canadian residents will be charged applicable provincial taxes and GST. Offer not valid in Quebec. This offer is limited to one order per household. All orders subject to approval. Credit or debit balances in a customer's account(s) may be offset by any other outstanding balance owed by or to the customer. Please allow 4 to 6 weeks for delivery. Offer available while quantities last.

Your Privacy: Silhouette Books is committed to protecting your privacy. Our Privacy Policy is available online at www.eHarlequin.com or upon request from the Reader Service. From time to time we make our lists of customers available to reputable third parties who may have a product or service of interest to you. If you would prefer we not share your name and address, please check here. ☐

SDES09R

Stay up-to-date on all your romance reading news!

HARLEQUIN free

Inside ROMANCE

APR | MAY | JUNE 2009

CELEBRATE 60 YEARS OF PURE READING PLEASURE WITH MORE EXCITING SERIES SPOTLIGHTS, FEATURED **EVERY MONTH!**

NEW YORK TIMES BESTSELLING AUTHOR **DIANA PALMER** BRINGS YOU A BRAND-NEW STORY!

CELEBRATE **MOTHER'S DAY** WITH HARLEQUIN®!

HARLEQUIN 60 · Silhouette

The Harlequin Inside Romance newsletter is a **FREE** quarterly newsletter highlighting our upcoming series releases and promotions!

Go to eHarlequin.com/InsideRomance or e-mail us at InsideRomance@Harlequin.com to sign up to receive your FREE newsletter today!

You can also subscribe by writing to us at: HARLEQUIN BOOKS Attention: Customer Service Department P.O. Box 9057, Buffalo, NY 14269-9057

Please allow 4-6 weeks for delivery of the first issue by mail.

IRNBPAQ209

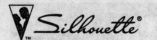
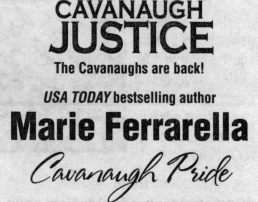

In 2009 Harlequin celebrates
60 years of pure reading pleasure!

We're marking this occasion by offering
16 **FREE** full books to download and read.

Visit

www.HarlequinCelebrates.com

to choose from a variety of
great romance stories
that are absolutely **FREE!**

(Total approximate retail value of $60)

We invite you to visit and share the Web site
with your friends, family
and anyone who enjoys reading.

COMING NEXT MONTH
Available August 11, 2009

#1957 BOSSMAN BILLIONAIRE—Kathie DeNosky
Man of the Month
The wealthy businessman needs an heir. His plan: hire his
attractive assistant as a surrogate mother. Her condition: marriage.

**#1958 ONE NIGHT WITH THE WEALTHY RANCHER—
Brenda Jackson**
Texas Cattleman's Club: Maverick County Millionaires
Unable to deny the lingering sparks with the woman he once
rescued, he's still determined to keep his distance…until her life is
once again in danger.

#1959 SHEIKH'S BETRAYAL—Alexandra Sellers
Sons of the Desert
Suspicious of his former lover's true motives, the sheikh sets out
to discover what brought her back to the desert. But soon it's
unclear who's seducing whom….

#1960 THE TYCOON'S SECRET AFFAIR—Maya Banks
The Anetakis Tycoons
A surprise pregnancy is not what this tycoon had in mind after one
blistering night of passion. Yet he insists on marrying his former
assistant…until a paternity test changes everything.

**#1961 BILLION-DOLLAR BABY BARGAIN—
Tessa Radley**
Billionaires and Babies
Suddenly co-guardians of an orphaned baby, they disliked each
other from the start. Until their marriage of convenience flares
with attraction impossible to deny….

#1962 THE MAGNATE'S BABY PROMISE—Paula Roe
This eligible bachelor must marry and produce an heir to keep
the family business. So when he discovers a one-night stand is
pregnant, nothing will get in his way of claiming the baby—and
the woman—as his own.

SDCNMBPA0709